The Misadventures of the
Broccoli Gang

In the Mystery of "Old Man Harlow"

Marquita Facen

NEWMAN SPRINGS PUBLISHING
320 Broad Street
Red Bank, NJ 07701

First originally published by Newman Springs Publishing 2020

ISBN 978-1-64801-755-1 (Paperback)
ISBN 978-1-64801-756-8 (Digital)

Printed in the United States of America

This book is dedicated to my childhood love of
mysteries and exploration in addition to all those that
read and loved this initial book. I thank you.

Q

CHAPTER 1

The Beginning

As all stories begin, once upon a time, there were three little boys who only wanted to play and ride their bikes—no no no that would be an inappropriate beginning for these boys. These boys, ages nine, ten, and eleven, were quite unique because they were not a gang as their name suggested, you know, like a bunch of mean-spirited kids who beat upon smaller kids. No, these three boys liked to have adventures, either real or imaginary.

Let us begin with our boys. First, there is the brain behind the trio, and he is the youngest at nine; his name is Richie Ruiz. Our second boy is the brawn. He too has a clever mind, but he has muscles, so children are a little bit intimidated by him. He is ten, and his name is Kevin McNeal. The third boy just happened to be at the right place at the right time. He was running from some bullies, who were trying to take his basketball, and ran smack into both Richie and Kevin, so Kevin saved his skin. He has been friends with them ever since. He is eleven, quite clever when he is not scared, and has a knack for fixing things. His name is Dell McPhearson.

From that moment, the boys were never apart from each other except for when they were at home. They saw each other during recess at school and were always trying to find a better way to stir up trouble, although they weren't troublemakers. The three always seem to be at the center of some adventure, whether they wanted to be or not. Since they all went to the same primary school and lived within blocks of each other, they always saw one another.

However, Saturday was their time to play from sun up to sun down, exploring the world on their bicycles. Their mothers respectively always packed them a lunch, usually a sandwich of some sort, a fruit, a vegetable (which the boys loathed), a juice or water bottle, and some type of goodie. The boys would have preferred a goodie and a juice box, and no vegetable, no matter how good they were for you. But they weren't the ones making the lunch, their "health conscious" parents were.

On one Saturday when they were out exploring by the old abandoned quarry, for the hundredth time, they stopped for lunch.

The quarry was an old limestone site. It had many burrows for the boys to explore, and they had been through about half of them. The burrows only went in for about thirty feet and were filled with tiny pieces of sharp and jagged limestone. The quarry had been closed in the early 1980s due to poor working conditions and safety standards. Several miners had been killed by overmining in certain sections and unstable support beams, this had led to the collapse of one of the burrows, it killed five men and injured a dozen more.

Their small rural town of Penskee, Wyoming, had taken a hard blow with this closure, and most of the miners and their families had moved to find jobs out of the state. With the mass exit of all the miners, the local economy was severely affected. The men in the town usually worked in the quarries, and their wives generally worked in the town's small textile factories along the old gravel road. As a result of the miners leaving, the textile companies closed shop soon afterward and left their abandoned buildings to rot slowly in the brash Wyoming heat.

However, in the mid '90s, a reconstruction effort began, and several big corporations came to town and brought with them hope and a new rebirth for their small town. Penskee was rapidly developing into a wonderful community, but it still had its small-time feel. Nevertheless, it was becoming more modern with new housing developments and a brand-new shopping mall in the works. They were becoming a little city now, and everyone in their town was enjoying the success.

There were also a lot of new people from all over the country moving to this town, and Penskee was becoming their own little melting pot of different cultures. The population had increased by fifty percent in the last ten years. As a result, they had to build a new primary school for all the children that came into the town. This is how the boys came to live in this great town, for their parents had all moved here to start a new life with new possibilities. They all found it here in Penskee, Wyoming, and none of them ever wanted to leave.

Penskee, Wyoming, was located some fifty miles south of the Devil's Tower, a national monument. The nickname for this town was dust bowl, for it was always blowing dust and dirt over everything. During the school year, the school district always arranged a trip to the monument, so the boys were looking forward to this, as was all the children in Penskee.

As the three boys were sitting there talking about the upcoming yearly carnival coming to town, they opened their lunch bags; they all discovered that their moms had packed broccoli for their vegetable. They all yelled at the same time then looked at each other and fell into a bunch of giggling kids.

Dell thought how dare his mother knowingly pack broccoli when she knows that it is his least favorite vegetable in the history of vegetables. As the boys lay there talking in the shade of the cave to the right of the quarry, Kevin had one of his brilliant moments when he suggested that they come up with a name for their little group.

"There are only three of us," said Dell.

"And your point?"

"Well, don't there have to be more than five to have a name of a group or something?"

"Umm, no, most groups start with two to three members then they get more to join."

"Okay, so we are trying to get people to join then."

"Maybe, if they are as smart as us." Kevin laughed.

"Yeah, that would be awesome. How about the biker gang?" said Richie.

"The biker gang," said Dell, shaking his head. "Are you crazy? As if we ride on motorcycles."

The other two looked at Dell and said together, "Umm, Dell, we ride on bicycles, hence the word *bikes*, as in biker gang."

"Oh."

"Well, anyways, how about something that we all like or dislike, such as this nasty, little, green piece of bushy-looking broccoli," as Richie was attempting to bury it in the dirt. However, he picked it up off the floor and looked at it, and then showed it to the other two, and they were just disgusted by it.

"Has there ever been an organization with a vegetable name?" asked Kevin.

Richie and Dell both looked at each other and then at Kevin and replied, "No."

"Hey, I got it, the BLT gang." Richie giggled.

"No, no, the PB and J gang." Dell laughed.

Kevin began to grin and giggle and grabbed the broccoli out of Dell's hand and held it up and said, "How about this piece of broccoli, my friends?"

Richie and Dell looked at Kevin with big smiles on their faces and thought the idea was brilliant. Therefore, their name was going to be the Broccoli Gang.

CHAPTER 2

The Abandoned House

On their way home from their afternoon of riding, sightseeing, and general horseplay, they decided to take the old gravel road home. This road led past several old abandoned houses.

All the houses seem to date back to the early 1940s and 1950s. A few were old colonial style, and the rest were on the order of ranch houses, but they were all in very bad shape. They should have been torn down years ago; however, no one ever came to this side of town except to throw stuff away. Across the road there were old factories from several textile plants, which were closed years ago. This whole area needed demolishing; it just didn't fit in with the town's reconstruction look.

Normally this ride is a cool breeze past the old roadside signs and the trash heaps where everybody dumped unwanted furniture and appliances (against the law, mind you). However, this was the place to ride free; no cars or trucks for them to watch out for.

The boys thought of themselves as explorers always on the lookout for something to do or get into. The three were riding home talking and laughing about their new name, when Dell spotted something out of the corner of his eye. He thought he was seeing things. As he slowed down his pedaling, he saw it again. An unknown person was coming out of one of the abandoned homes carrying a rather large package. This piqued Dell's interest, so he called to the guys and told them to wait up; he needed to tell them something. When he finally caught up to them, he told them what he had seen.

Kevin and Richie looked at each other and said, "Sure, Dell, you saw a strange man carrying a large package."

"Was it a man covered in fur?" asked Kevin seriously.

"No," said Dell with a wrinkled brow.

"You know they have had a few sightings of Bigfoot around here lately," said Richie, trying not to laugh out loud.

"But I did see it."

As they kept on riding, he looked behind him and saw the man go back into the house and close the door. Dell was about to say something else but decided to let it go, and they continued their journey home. By the time they got home it was late, well past their 5:00 p.m. curfew, and their parents were highly upset with them. So quite naturally, the boys were grounded for a month, of no riding their bikes.

The next day after school, they all sat on Kevin's porch and asked what they should do this summer, since they only had one month of school left.

Dell suggested that they go exploring out around the old abandoned houses. Because he just could not forget about that strange character he had seen going into that house. The other boys were thinking that maybe they wanted to go fishing down by Green River Lake or go to the amusement park to play miniature golf, or just do nothing for the next two and a half months. However, Dell had other ideas and hoped that his best friends would want to tag along on this new adventure.

One month later, the last day of school, their parents granted them a curfew of 7:00 p.m. It was still going to be light out, so they would not be worried about the kids during the daylight hours. The boys promised to be back by 6:59 p.m. So off they went riding, and the first place Dell steered them toward was the old abandoned homes. However, both Richie and Kevin were against it, but Dell promised them both a new packet of basketball cards, the gold edition with a guaranteed hologram card inside. They immediately said yes, for they were serious basketball card collectors and always either playing basketball or watching it.

As they began riding along the gravel road, they came upon several vacant houses. Dell led them to the one that he saw the man come out of. They got off their bikes, parked them next to the stairs, sneaked up to the front porch, and did not notice anything out of order. There was still dust and cobwebs on the door and across the porch; it looked as if it needed repair. Some of the boards were rotted away, and the front door was hanging by a thread. There was also an old porch swing that looked as if you were to think about sitting on it, it would go through the rotted wood on the porch, directly into the basement.

"You have got to be crazy, Dell," said Richie.

"Come on, you two, you came this far."

Ritchie and Kevin said, "No way are we going in there, it doesn't look safe."

"Sure it is. It only *looks* unsafe."

The other two rolled their eyes at Dell and said, "Okay, let's check it out."

While they were about to enter the front door, they heard movement in the house and a scuffling noise like someone was inside moving furniture.

They ran off the porch and hid behind some trees, and then Kevin said, "What about the bikes?"

They all ran to get their bikes and move them behind a wood pile that was stacked up to the side of the house by some trees. The boys waited what seemed like an eternity for someone to come out, and when he did, they were speechless.

CHAPTER 3

Old Man Harlow

It was Old Man Harlow, who was supposed to be dead. The boys were in shock. They had grown up seeing pictures and hearing the old tale of how Old Man Harlow bit the dust. Every time their parents took them to get a haircut, the old-timers in the shop always ended up talking about Old Man Harlow and his claim to fame. The barber shop had old pictures of him on the mirrors, and the bulletin boards had newspaper clippings about him, among other things. He was the talk of late Saturday night gossip, even after all these years.

It was a late summer night when Old Man Harlow went fishing on Green River Lake, and suddenly, out of nowhere, a summer storm had appeared. Instead of him coming into dock his boat, he stayed out there *fishing*. The storm became so violent that his boat capsized, and he was thrown overboard.

The waves were crashing and tossing him around in the lake. He supposedly swam ashore, and as he took refuge under a tree, shivering with the cold wind that was going through his wet clothes touching his body, out of the sky came a horrifying sound; it was the sound of thunder and lightning. Old Man Harlow looked up, and before he could run from under the tree, a massive bolt of lightning struck him, and it sent him flying in the air a good hundred feet. He landed in a pile of metal tire rims, where a couple taking a walk around the lake later found his body.

They only found him because of the stench of the body; he had been there for four days. Nobody reported him missing because he kept to himself and was considered a loner. The only time people in the small town of Penskee saw him was when he was going to the grocery store, hardware store, or to the local post office.

Most of the townsfolk always saw him on the lake fishing, but he never spoke to anyone, never gave eye contact. So after his body was found, the town sponsored his funeral. Everyone came to pay their respects, and he was buried in the local cemetery with a nice granite headstone, which was donated by the city council. Old Man Harlow was no more…until now.

As the boys were pedaling home from their discovery, they wondered who to tell and if they should tell someone. Who would believe them? So they decided to keep it to themselves for now and figure out what he was doing there in that old abandoned house. Dell also wondered what was in the package that he saw him with. It was decided that their summer was going to be in discovering the truth behind Old Man Harlow and his supposed death.

The next morning was a bright, hot Saturday morning, and all three boys met at Richie's house to talk about their strategy in investigating Old Man Harlow. Since they had the entire day until 7:00 p.m., they wanted to use their daylight hours spending as much time they could watching the old house. Therefore, what they came up with was ways to do a series of ride-bys, at different times of the day, to see if they could catch any sign of him. After they would catch him, then they would plot some strategy to get into the house. However, this plan was harder than they imagined.

On their first day of starting the plan, they rode past the house at 8:00 a.m., then again at noon, and finally at 5:00 p.m., but they saw no sign of Old Man Harlow. So they decided on the following day to break up the pattern and ride on the hour, each boy taking turns, then writing down their results in their notebooks. Once they agreed on this plan, it was put into effect. Richie would ride past the house first at 8:00 a.m., then Kevin at 9:00 a.m., and Dell at 10:00 a.m.; they would follow this pattern taking turns until 7:00 p.m.

They rode and rode until their legs felt like they were going to fall off. When Dell pulled up to Kevin's house at 7:25 p.m., they compared notes on today's activities and came up with some amazing news. During Richie's ride at 8:00 a.m., he noticed the front door open on the abandoned house, and he saw a shadow of somebody dragging something across the front room; however, he could not make out any faces. On Kevin's ride at noon, he too saw a shadow throwing something into what looked like a pit; he thought it was garbage. He knew he needed to get a look at that garbage, but not now, maybe later or at some other time. As Dell rode by at 4:00 p.m., he saw Old Man Harlow outside covered in a long trench coat with a hat burning something in a pit alongside the house. Dell knew that he had to come back and search that burnt pile of trash, but when was going to be the problem.

As the boys compared notes on what they had seen, they knew that something was going on in that house. The boys needed to get to that garbage pit and see what he was burning, and lastly, they needed to get inside the house to further see what Old Man Harlow was up to.

CHAPTER 4

Getting into the House

As the boys sat around on the following Tuesday morning rehashing what they had learned about Old Man Harlow over the weekend, they continued their talk on how to get into the house. So as they got ready to leave and go watch the house again, Kevin's mom, Mrs. McNeal, ran out to give him his lunch for the day, and she asked the others if they have lunch.

"No," they said.

"I wish I had brought a lunch with me, but I forgot," said Dell in his sweetest voice.

Richie piped up, "Me too, but I was in such a rush to come and visit Kevin that I too forgot to pack a lunch."

Mrs. McNeal laughed. "You two don't fool me one bit with all that sly talk. Do you boys want me to make you a lunch as well? It would be no problem."

"Yes, ma'am!"

Mrs. McNeal went in and made them the same lunch she had made Kevin. It was toasted peanut butter and jelly sandwich with carrot sticks, a chewy granola bar, a juice box, and bottled water. All three boys thanked her, and they headed off to spy on Old Man Harlow.

The boys had to find a place in order to spy without being seen by anybody in the house or any other people that might pass by. They spotted one of the old factories across the street and decided to go and see if it was safe enough to hide inside of it. They went to the one directly across from the house. It sat back off the road a good seventy-five feet; it had a perfect view of the front and sides of the house.

The inside of the factory was in a horrible state. There were old desks, lockers, giant weaving machines, pieces of fabric, broken glass from windows, and spools of rotting thread all over the floor. The sign on the ground said, "Turner's Textiles Incorporated." The boys knew that it had, at one time, been a factory that made rugs and quilts, by the looks of all the discarded pieces of rugs and reams of tattered fabrics.

The boys cleared a section near the front door that had a big old-fashioned round window that would be a perfect spying tool. It even came covered in an old ratty checkered curtain. The boys found a few chairs and a table and set it up in front of the window. They found a place to park their bikes inside, and they began to watch the house. Since it was around lunchtime, the boys ate their lunches that Mrs. McNeal had made, and all agreed that it was delicious. Around 1:00 p.m. they saw Old Man Harlow leave. He climbed into an old navy blue '57 Chevy truck with tinted windows. The boys had never seen this truck before today, because it was hidden under a brown tarp, which looked like a pile of old used rags.

"So that is why we couldn't see the truck. He had it hidden," said Dell.

As he left, the boys decided it was now or never to enter the house.

They left their bikes in the factory and ran across the crunchy gravel road to the house.

As the boys were running across the road, they could really see the house. It was a three-story old colonial house with a wraparound porch. It had a small front door, but on either side of it were two big bay windows covered in newspapers that were starting to fall off from the inside. Right above the entrance to the front door hung a sign, 3254 Beacon Road; under the address was the name McKenzie, and it was a large wooden sign that had weathered with age.

The old house was painted a dark green with white trim, but with time and age, the paint had begun to chip and peel. All the windows had shutters and were closed on all the levels and were in good condition. They could tell that the house had a basement from the windows that looked like they were in the dirt, but they too were covered in newspaper that was falling off. As the boys looked up, there was a decorative type of steeple on top of the attic it almost looked like an old church. The house would have been a beautiful colonial if it was fully restored.

Once they got to the front door and found that it was locked, they began to check all the first-floor windows; however, none of the windows would open.

"Shoot," said Richie, "something has to be open around here."

They went around to the back door, and they tried it to, but it was locked also.

They were about to give up when Richie spotted a basement window that was cracked open a notch.

"Here, over here," yelled Richie. "This basement window might be our ticket in to this house."

The boys went to the window and pried it open, but it was only big enough for a super thin person to fit through. They all looked at each other and began measuring; it was obvious the only one that could fit was Kevin.

"I guess it's going to be me. I will hurry and open the front door so that we all can search the house before Old Man Harlow gets back," said Kevin.

Richie and Dell nodded in agreement and told him to be careful. Then Kevin snuck in through the window. The other boys went back around to the front porch and waited anxiously for him to open the door.

When Kevin entered the basement, he immediately looked around; since it was dark in there, it took a minute for his eyes to adjust to the darkness. He began to feel around while his eyes adjusted and felt old soggy clothes and paper, a lot of paper.

When his eyes finally adjusted, he saw the old moldy clothes he had been touching and the piles upon piles of old newspapers and magazines. It smelled disgusting in here; the smell was coming from the water-soaked papers, clothes, and old garbage bags that had been thrown in here.

Kevin just knew that there were rats down there, and the one thing he hated more than broccoli was rats. He began looking for a door, and out of the corner of his eye he saw a glint of something shiny on one of the paneled walls. But first, he had to find the door to get out and to let his friends in. As he looked up, he saw the door, and he had to climb over more garbage bags to get to the stairs that led to the door.

He climbed the stairs, and when he got to the top, he put his hand on the knob and began to turn it slowly; at the very same time, someone from the other side began to turn the knob also. Kevin jumped off the stairs directly into the garbage bags he had just climbed over to get to the stairs, and he fell into something very squishy.

"This has got to be the worst smell in the history of smells," said Kevin as he rolled off the bags, hid behind them, and shook what looked like moldy mashed potatoes off his hands and pant legs.

The person that opened the door looked down the stairs and saw nothing but darkness. He began to go down the stairs but stopped, went back up, and closed the door behind him. Kevin got up and went back to the window and, using a book case under the window, climbed out; this search would have to continue another day.

CHAPTER 5

A New Plan

After Kevin got out of the basement window, he ran around to the front of the house and hid in a bunch of shrubs that were in front of the porch. He saw that the '57 Chevy truck had indeed returned. Kevin began to panic while looking over the hedge for his friends. First, he turned, looked on the porch, and didn't see them.

"Where could they be?" asked Kevin.

He looked across the road at the old factory and didn't see any signs of them. Then he heard something very faint. He listened hard while looking around. He heard it again, someone calling his name. It was Dell, calling his name in a whisper, "Kevin, Kevin over here." Kevin saw them behind the wood pile off to the side of the house. He ran to them, and they were all relieved to be all right. They scampered back across the gravel road; it felt like they were running on ice chips it made so much noise to their ears.

Once they got inside the factory, they fell on their chairs and rested their heads on the table. The boys couldn't believe what they had done without really thinking it through. Next time they would be more prepared. Instead of all three going in next time, maybe they would have a lookout so as not to have this happen again.

After they rode home it was around four in the afternoon, and they went to Dell's house to talk about what had happened and what went wrong at Old Man Harlow's. Dell began by asking Kevin what he saw in the basement.

Kevin said, "Man, I don't ever want to go in there again. It smelled horrible. It smelled like your old sweaty socks, Dell."

"Oh, you got jokes." Dell laughed.

"Okay, you two. Now tell us what you saw in the basement, Kevin," said Richie.

"There were piles and piles of moldy clothes and newspapers. I even fell into some old garbage bags that had old mashed potatoes in it, when I jumped off the stairs."

"Disgusting," said Dell with a shiver.

"Was there gravy?" said Richie.

The boys held their laughs as they investigated Kevin's face and saw that he was really disgusted by the whole basement.

"Oh," said Kevin, "there was this interesting glare coming off one of the panels in the basement. It looked like a hole or something. I couldn't get to it. There were newspapers piled in front of the wall; it would have taken forever to move by myself."

"We need to get back in there," said Richie.

"I know, I know," said Dell, "but we have to have a solid plan this time and a proper escape route in case Old Man Harlow comes back home too soon."

Kevin then asked, "What happened to you guys on the porch, while I was inside the basement?"

Richie told him, "We waited on the porch, which seemed like days, and then we began to hear the sound of the truck coming back."

Dell picked up the story and said, "We were not sure if it was the '57 Chevy truck or not, so we hid behind the wood pile under the tarp until we could be sure of whom it was. As soon as the truck pulled up, me and Richie ran to the shed next to the porch and hid behind that.

"It was a good thing we did," said Richie, "because as soon as Old Man Harlow got out, he went straight for the tarp to cover his truck."

Dell jumped in finishing, "We watched as Old Man Harlow took packages into the house. We didn't know if we should rush in and save you or run for it. When we decided to go for help, you came sneaking from the side of the house. Let me tell you, we were so happy to see you."

After they had each finished telling their tales of what happened, they decided that Old Man Harlow had to be followed the next time they were watching him. The boys also knew that they needed walkie-talkies to talk to one another if they are split up again. These walkie-talkies had to have at least a fifteen-mile range.

Dell told them he would look into getting the walkie-talkies because his dad worked for an electronics firm that specializes in communications equipment. His dad was always bringing home equipment to test out.

Richie said, "I'll research the old colonial house and Old Man Harlow on the internet or at the library to see if indeed this was him, or if he had any living relatives who might resemble him."

"I know what job I get," said Kevin. "I get stuck with the boring task of watching the house and following Old Man Harlow. I hope that he is a slow driver so that I can follow him on my bike, because I can't drive."

The other two boys turned and faced each other and rolled their eyes at Kevin's remarks. They all agreed to meet at Kevin's house a week from Saturday to discuss whatever information they found and maybe begin to piece together this puzzle.

CHAPTER 6

Surprising Information

One week later they met at Kevin's house, and each has some interesting information for the meeting. Kevin's mom made them sandwiches and juice pops. As they settled on the porch to talk, they saw the old '57 Chevy drive by very slowly, and the man driving was staring at them as if he knew them. They all looked at one another and felt shivers go up and down their spines.

After he drove by, the boys got into what they found out from their assignments. First up was Dell. He told the boys that his dad had three walkie-talkies that had a range of twenty-five miles; they were prototypes for his company.

"The best part is my dad told me that we can use them in exchange for helping him clean out our garage later on in the summer," said Dell. He continued, "I agreed to the terms and told my father that all of us would have no problem with that."

The boys rolled their eyes, but Dell didn't quite notice it.

Little did Dell know was that the two boys, Richie and Kevin, hated to clean anything, but for the sake of the walkie-talkies, they nodded in agreement, when Dell told them the news.

Richie had four pages of notes on the research he had done about the house and Old Man Harlow. He went to the library to search old newspapers for any clippings about the house or the man; he also searched the internet for any information. What he found out was surprising to the other two boys. First, he found out that Old Man Harlow was in fact dead.

Richie passed around a newspaper clipping and continued reading.

Richie said, "The fact that he was dead was confirmed by this photo that was printed over thirty years ago in 1975 by the local newspaper, *The Trident*. It was taken after his body was found by the couple taking a walk around the lake."

Dell cut in, "So who's that man that looks just like him?"

"Hold on," said Richie.

Richie continued, "He was around seventy years old at the time of his death, and he had an ex-wife and a son from the marriage, with whom he had no contact."

All the boys looked at one another with puzzled looks on their faces and then began to read the newspaper article that Richie had found.

According to *The Trident*, "Old Man Harlow or Harlow McKenzie was a suspect in several bank robberies in the early 1950s in the town of Pine Haven, Wyoming, which is about fifty miles west of the town of Penskee, Wyoming. He was also a suspect in a couple of others in nearby towns as well." It goes on to say, "Harlow McKenzie was a local troublemaker with a history of petty thefts and was suspected immediately in the five bank robberies of the National Trust Bank of Wyoming. These robberies went on for about five years, with no real suspects. All five banks lost a combined total of approximately $750,000 to $1,000,000 dollars. There was never an exact total because the banks did not keep accurate records. The money was never found, and Harlow McKenzie was never tried or arrested, just questioned and released."

Angus Feltwater, a crime reporter for *The Trident*, wrote, "Although his home on 3254 Beacon Road was searched many times, the money was never found. At the time of his death in 1975, he lived alone and collected glass bottles. He would cash the bottles in for money. If he did rob the banks, he never spent a lot of the money at one time. Old Man Harlow was seen on the regular at the grocery and hardware store. However, he lived his life as a pauper. He died a poor, lonely old man who never had a chance to see his only son grow up to become a master criminal as well. In this town, to all the townspeople, he remained guilty of the bank robberies."

Dell jumped up and said, "So it's his son! Man, he looks just like his dad."

As Richie collected the articles they had just read, they sat there and shook their heads.

Richie then gasped, "Oh my gosh, all that noise we heard and the packages he's bringing in the house are all for one thing."

Kevin and Dell were staring at him while he was talking, then Kevin said, "What is he looking for?"

"The money, he's looking for the stolen money," said Richie.

"You have to be kidding," said Dell.

"But what was he burning on the side of the house in the garbage pit?" said Kevin.

They all looked at one another and knew that they had to check out the burnt things in the garbage pit.

After they had a few minutes to digest all the information that Richie had, it was Kevin's turn to report on his week's activities.

Kevin told them where the son went on the days that he followed him. On Monday he went to the hardware store; he bought a pick, shovel, and some gloves. Tuesday, he followed him to the army surplus store, where he purchased some night goggles and a portable building X-ray machine.

"Thank goodness he dropped his receipt because I didn't know what to call that X-ray machine thing. I thought it was a generator," said Kevin.

Kevin continued with his report. "On Wednesday he stayed home, but I heard a lot of noise coming from the house. I stayed near the basement window so he couldn't see me. Thursday, he went to the grocery store and bought food and lottery tickets.

"On Friday he went to the post office and picked up a package and a letter. He was so excited that he opened the letter on his way out and began to laugh and do a little dance as if the letter contained great news for him. People on the sidewalk just thought he was another crazy person talking to himself."

Kevin told the boys, "It seemed like the son was up to something, and whatever it was, it was not good."

The other boys nodded their heads in agreement.

CHAPTER 7

A Discovery at the Library

The boys spent the next week just acting like they were on vacation, although they each kept on thinking about the old house out on Beacon Road. They decided to take this time to relax and go fishing. The boys knew they had to come up with a way to search the house while the son was out. While fishing, Dell came up with an idea, and his ideas were normally very good ones, so the boys put down their poles and listened.

"What we need are blueprints or plans to the house, because if the police searched his house and didn't find anything, then he must have built a secret room or had hidden areas in the house. Those secrets might be on the plans," said Dell.

"Well," said Kevin, "why would you put hidden places on a blueprint? Then the world would know you had built secret chambers in your house. If I was hiding something, I wouldn't show or tell people about it."

"Yeah, that's a good point, but this was some fifty years ago. Maybe people didn't pay attention to things like that, the way they would now," said Dell.

Richie said, "My dad told me once that while he was in a contractor's office waiting for some paperwork, a man walked in and wanted to know if he could put something into a wall that was already built without drawing up new plans. He wanted to put in a secret safe that was to be in a wall. In order to do this, the architect had to redraw the wall with the safe in it so they could submit it for approval." He continued, "Whenever you do upgrades on a house or building, you have to get a new set of blueprints for the existing building to let the contractor know where to put in the item that you want."

Kevin looked at him and said, "But Old Man Harlow would not want anyone to see that he had hidden the money in a secret chamber, let alone make blueprints for it."

"Possibly, he had the blueprints redrawn and just submitted them to the county contractor's office, and the contractor didn't give them a second thought. This is a small town. Who is going to pay attention to a man whom the town considers a loner who collects glass bottles?" said Dell.

Richie said, "Maybe he paid someone in the contractor's office to keep quiet about the changes in the house. You never know. He had a lot of money to throw around at people to keep their mouths shut."

"I still say that Old Man Harlow would not have been that silly as to put his hiding places on paper," said Kevin with his arms folded across his chest.

Dell saw that they were getting ready to argue and jumped in and said, "Let's not get ahead of ourselves just yet. Let's find out how to get blueprints first before we start to argue, okay, guys."

The other two agreed and tried to figure out where they would start looking for the blueprints as Dell kept trying to fish.

They had to get the building plans without the help of grown-ups, but getting the blueprints without a grown-up knowing what they were up to would be a challenge.

Each boy asked their parents casually during dinner how they would go about getting blueprints for a building in town. All their parents thought this was an odd subject for small talk at the dinner table, but they each gave some type of suggestion on how to go about it.

Richie's dad, Mr. Ruiz, suggested that he would go to the town supervisor's office to obtain a set of blueprints.

Richie said, "Okay, thanks for the information, Dad," although he didn't think that was the way the boys wanted to go about it.

Dell's dad, Mr. McPhearson, told Dell, "I would go to the city council and ask for help there."

"Oh, the city council, I would have never had thought of that, Dad. Thanks for the information," said Dell, but he didn't think that was the way to do it either.

Kevin's dad, Mr. McNeal, said, "In some towns or cities, most blueprints were kept online and that the local library had access to those sites. All you have to do is print them out, and it's free of charge in most libraries."

Kevin told his dad, "Thanks for the information, Dad."

Kevin couldn't wait to tell his friends the next day so they could see if it was true.

The next morning, as Kevin rode up to Richie's house followed by Dell, they all began to talk at once about what their fathers had told them about getting blueprints.

Only Mr. McNeal's suggestion was helpful to the boys in their opinion. Besides, it wouldn't raise suspicions with adults. If they were to walk into the city council or town's supervisor's office asking for this information, then they would have questions for the boys, and they couldn't chance that just yet. The library was quiet and open to the public, and they wouldn't have to talk to anyone but the librarian. The library was the best plan, and they were going to see if they could find Old Man Harlow's blueprints.

As they pedaled to the library, they saw the old '57 Chevy at the local hardware store. When they got to the library, they asked the librarian about the blueprints, and she pointed them to a computer with access to city records.

The librarian stared at them as they walked toward the public records computer, and she wondered what they could want with blueprints. But before she could ask them, someone came up to ask her a question about a book, so she forgot about them.

This computer was not like other computers. Its screen was at least thirty inches across, and it was like watching a television.

It had a standard keyboard, but a very large and round mouse. The librarian told them that all they had to do was to type in the address of the building, and when it comes up, just hit print and it will print out a set on the large printer for blueprints. After she left, Richie did the typing as he was clearly more computer savvy than the other two. He typed in the address 3254 Beacon Road, and there were two sets of prints. The first set of prints was from the year 1943, and a revision set of prints were for the year 1950, so they decided to print both.

Each set of blueprints consisted of fifteen pages each. As they approached the printer, they saw the sign that read the first two pages are free and twenty-five cents per page after that. The boys stopped in their tracks. They had brought no money with them. When they stopped at the printer, the librarian looked at the boys then at the amount of paper that had been used.

The librarian said, "You printed thirty pages and only four were free, you three owe the library $6.50."

"How do you boys expect to pay for this?" asked the librarian in an unfriendly tone. She really didn't care for children, especially children who used up her resources and couldn't pay for them.

Kevin piped up and said, "We were told this would be free of charge."

"Oh, were you?" said the librarian. "Well, it isn't. Now who has the money?"

The librarian was not pleased. She stood before them with her arms folded, glasses hanging off the edge of her nose, and the boys looked up slowly to meet her gaze. She indeed had a puzzled look on her face.

Dell explained that his dad worked a block over and asked if he could go and get the money.

"Make it snappy, young man. Coming in here using all the paper and not having the money to pay for it, the gall of you kids these days," said the librarian as she turned and walked back to her desk.

While Dell went to get the money, Kevin and Richie sat down and started looking at the blueprints. They split up the different sections of the house. Kevin took the attic, second floor, and kitchen, while Richie took the living room, first floor, and the basement, for starters. There were only about ten pages of actual blueprints for the house, the rest were contracts and correspondence between contractor, architect, and project manager.

Kevin spotted a difference in one of the walls in the attic and made a mark on the blueprint of the difference. The second floor and kitchen were identical to each other. Richie's prints were harder to read. There were some differences in the living room, but it looked as if it was confined to the stairs, or the wall behind the stairs, he was unsure. The first floor looked identical to one another, while the basement looked as if it had a false wall built on an existing wall, so he marked that area on the blueprint.

Just then Dell came running into the library and went right over to the librarian and paid her.

The librarian told him, "Never to come in here again without having the money," for she had been nice to let him go and get it, it won't happen again.

Dell smiled and said, "Well, ma'am, I really appreciate it, and next time we will bring some change with us, just in case we need to print something."

The boys were about to search the other prints of the bathroom and all three bedrooms.

Dell ran over to the table and said, "Hey, leave some for me."

He quickly searched his blueprints and found nothing out of the ordinary. The other two boys told Dell of their slight differences in their prints. They looked at each other and smiled.

"Now we know where things might be hidden in the house," said Richie.

Kevin asked, "Do you think the money will still be in good condition after all these years?"

"It should be," said Dell.

Richie spoke half to himself and to the boys, "I wonder if there is anything to be found. I mean the son has been in there for some time. What if he has found the money already?"

Both Kevin and Dell were wondering the same as Richie but just listened as he expressed the same worries they had.

The boys couldn't help but wonder if the son knew about these blueprints. Had he also been in here to retrieve them? They would never know the answer to those questions. All they knew was that they had to search the house and soon.

CHAPTER 8

In the House, Finally

After leaving the library, the boys decided that they would go in the old house the following Friday. They were hoping that the son was going to be out for a few hours. When Kevin followed him before, every time he went out it was always around two to three hours. They were hoping that he had somewhere to go on Friday. Their plan was to search the garbage pit first for any clues then go into the house. The only problem they had was to see which of them was going to keep an eye on the son while they were in the house. It was a good thing they had the walkie-talkies. Now they could try them out.

As they prepared for Friday, several bags were gathered for the money, in case they found it. They all took some tools such as a flathead screwdriver, hammer, flashlight, and pliers. All three boys emptied their school backpacks to put these items in. They also made sure that they had change for the payphone in case they had to call the local sheriff. They all met at Dell's at nine o'clock on Friday morning and immediately took off for the old house. As soon as they arrived, they saw the '57 Chevy truck and heard a lot of banging and ripping sounds. The boys knew that he was hard at work on destroying the inside of the house.

Once they heard the noise coming from the old house, they decided to wait inside the old textile factory across the road. The boys waited for two hours before the son decided to leave. Since Kevin had followed the son before, they all voted for him to continue to follow the son.

Kevin said, "Why do I have to follow him?"

Richie said, "Because you are the best at riding on streets without getting hit by a car."

Dell just looked at Richie and shook his head in agreement, because he was telling him the truth. He reached over and handed Kevin a walkie-talkie and told him to turn it to channel 5.

"Also, use it only in an emergency, because the battery doesn't last long the further out you go. I forgot to charge them last night, sorry," said Dell.

Kevin just looked at him and jumped on his bike and started off after the truck. He yelled back," You guys be careful."

The boys yelled the same to him as Kevin had to really pedal to keep up with the son.

"Why is he going so fast?" asked Kevin. It was hard trying to keep up with the old truck without being seen by him. However, Kevin did it by riding on the sidewalks and by riding behind other cars to hide himself.

Richie and Dell ran across the crunchy gravel road with their backpacks and went straight to the garbage pit and began poking around the ashes with a stick. They came across a letter with scorch marks throughout it. Someone had tried to burn it, but they were unsuccessful. From what Richie and Dell could make out, it had Harlow's name on it, the word *money*, and authorities on it.

The boys both looked at each other and said at the same time, "Oh my gosh."

The boys thought that this was suspicious, so they put the half-burnt letter into a little plastic bag they had brought with them. Dell went to the front door to see if it was open, and to his surprise it was unlocked.

He whispered to Richie, "Richie! Richie!"

"Why are you whispering?" said Richie.

"Oh...I don't know," said Dell with a light chuckle. "Hey, the door is unlocked, let's go."

As they entered, the house was in shambles. There were floor boards hacked up all over the place, the walls had holes in them, and even the ceiling had signs of being tampered with.

Dell sighed and said, "Man, he is serious about finding the money, huh, Richie?"

Richie looked at him and with a smile said, "Let's find it first."

Upon entering the old house, they decided to split up. Dell would go to the attic, and Richie would search the staircase. Dell found his way to the attic, almost falling through the floor on the upper landing. There was a big hole in the floor, and it was covered by a rug.

"Phew," said Dell, "that was close; I almost landed back in the living room with Richie."

Luckily for him he only had one leg on the rug when it gave way beneath him. As Dell made his way to the attic, Richie began exploring the staircase, looking for any hidden button or lever of some type to open up one of the steps or an opening on the wall behind the staircase, but no luck. He was on the third step with fifteen more to go.

"I have to hurry," said Richie.

With tires screeching, Kevin was following the son at a high rate of speed; his legs were beginning to cramp up. He had been pedaling for about twenty minutes nonstop as fast as he could to keep up with the son. Kevin was so relieved when he saw the truck pull into a local diner; he was going in for breakfast. Kevin thought this is just great. He can rest while the son eats, and by the looks of the line out the door waiting to be seated, he would be there for some time. The son got out of his truck and took his place in line.

Kevin parked on the other side of the concrete fence separating the diner and a gas station. He was well out of sight, so he radioed his friends to tell them what was going on.

"Hey guys, come in, this is Kevin," said Kevin.

"Yeah," said Dell. "You don't have to say your name." Dell laughed.

"Oh, right." Kevin laughed. "Just wanted you to know we are at the diner about three miles from the house. He is in line to be seated. Should be here for a while. Talk to you soon."

"Thanks," said Richie. "Stop talking like a robot, Kevin, all right."

"Okay, I thought it sounded like cool soldier talk." Kevin laughed.

"Roger, over and out," said Kevin.

"Over and out," said Richie, while he got back to searching his stairs.

Dell was working up a sweat in the attic as he was tapping the walls, trying not to get a splinter. He saw little notches in the wood on the wall facing him and went over to explore. When he put his finger in the hole, he felt something furry. He let out a little scream then immediately covered his mouth looking around, and told himself to get a grip, be a man, not a mouse, as his knees was shaking. He took the screwdriver, turned his head, closed his eyes, and stuck it in the hole, expecting there to be blood on it from what had felt like a fuzzy animal.

"No blood?" Dell asked, opening his squinting eyes to look at the clean screwdriver.

Dell saw that there was just enough room to fit the flat-head screwdriver between two boards. "Hmmm," thought Dell, "maybe I can pry the board away from the wall."

He began to pry the board loose, thinking, *What's the difference? The entire attic was ready to crumble.* It didn't take more than a few muscle pushes and the board flew off the wall. Dell had to duck because it would have hit him in the face.

When he looked up, he mouthed the word, "Wow."

After he stopped looking at what he had found, he finally found his voice and whispered, "I found the money! I found the money!"

He had found a stash of old, fuzzy, moldy money he could not believe it. He radioed the other two to tell him what he had found, and Kevin could not believe it. He wished he was there instead of following the son.

Richie was yelling from downstairs, "Put it all in the bag, no matter how moldy it is, and then put that bag in your backpack."

Dell started putting the moldy, squishy, falling-apart money in the bag.

"Ewww...why do I get all the dirty jobs?" asked Dell.

Downstairs things were not going as smoothly as the attic. Richie was having a difficult time locating anything that looked like it held a secret compartment. However, he kept looking and looking and looking. Step after step after step. He was ready to call it quits when something caught his eye on step fourteen. He turned and looked at all the other steps. They were all the same except for the fourteenth step. He looked above that step at the remaining three steps and found that those were the same as the ones below him. His step was different. Maybe this is what he was looking for.

Richie began to run his hand over the stair and the lip of the stair; he felt nothing, at first. He ran his hand over the step again, and when he got to the upper right corner of the stair, he noticed a small hole. His finger was too big, so he fished out his screwdriver and it fit perfectly. Richie moved it around and there was a spring-like sound, and the step popped up revealing a secret hollow compartment. As he looked in the space, there was a letter still sealed in an envelope, a silver baby rattle, and a solid heart-shaped necklace. Richie carefully placed all items in the plastic bag that he had placed the burnt letter in.

Suddenly, over the radio, Kevin was yelling, "He's coming back, he's coming back. The diner was too crowded, I guess. He stormed out angry, he took off, and he is driving really fast. I can barely keep up with him. Get out fast and get to the factory; he is on Main Street five blocks from the house."

"Oh my gosh," screamed Dell from up above.

"Hurry up and get down here, Dell," yelled Richie.

Richie yelled up to Dell, "Put the board back as best you can and get down here now."

Dell didn't need to reply; he had just packed the last of the squishy money in the bag and was putting the board back when Kevin came over the walkie-talkie. Now Richie was yelling at him to hurry. He thought to himself he was going to have a heart attack with all this yelling. He put his tools and money bag in the backpack he didn't even zip it up. Dell began to sprint down the second-floor landing, jumped over the hole in the floor, and met Richie closing the stair he had opened.

"All set?" said Richie.

"Yep," said Dell.

"We will have to search the basement tomorrow or some other day," said Dell.

"Uh-huh, but let's run for now," said Richie.

They took off making sure they closed the door and ran as fast as they could across the crunchy gravel road to the factory. They left not a moment too soon, for as they stepped in the doorway of the textile factory, the boys saw his truck rounding the corner at breakneck speed. They saw Kevin right behind him hunched over his handlebars, and he tore across the field, heading for the factory.

The boys got out of his way as he sped into the factory door and crashed into an old desk. The other two boys closed the door as quickly as he had entered and went to go and check on Kevin. He was fine; he hopped off his bike and went to the window, just in time to see the son parking his truck and putting the tarp on it.

Kevin closed the curtain, turned, and said with a big smile, "We did it."

Dell could have fainted on the spot, and Richie looked at Kevin and smiled and said, "Yes, we did. However, we didn't get to the basement; that will have to wait for another time."

They looked out the window to make sure the coast was clear. As they opened the door to the factory, hopped on their bikes, and began to ride home, they were nervous, sweaty, and scared. They had just pulled off a major discovery. Although the basement had not been searched, they could enter it from the outside if they had to. That task was for another day, maybe tomorrow. Who knows?

Once they searched the basement, they would have the whole story concerning this man. Hopefully this mystery would be solved before the end of their summer vacation. They had less than a month left, and they really wanted to spend some of it doing nothing. But on the other hand, the boys couldn't wait to see what it was that they had discovered and what this discovery might have on their small little town.

CHAPTER 9

Sifting through Memories

As soon as they left Beacon Road, they pedaled as fast as their legs could carry them. They had to get to the nearest house and fast. It proved to be Richie's house.

It was around 12:30 p.m., and Richie's mom, Mrs. Ruiz, was making lunch and asked the boys if they wanted some lunch.

All three boys had not realized that they were starving, probably because of the adrenaline rush of pedaling so fast.

Richie told his mom, "Yes, we will take whatever you are making. We are starving."

His mom said, "Whatever, huh?" because she knows he is a picky eater, so she made them grilled cheese sandwiches, broccoli with ranch, a small bag of chips, and a bottled water. The boys ate without complaint, even the dreaded broccoli. After they were finished, they thanked her for lunch, and then they went to get their belongings.

They knew they had to go back to the house within a few days to search the basement. Since they had found things in the other two places of the house, it was only obvious that something was hidden in the basement.

They took their bikes and bags around to the back porch, where they would not be seen. Now, to see what they had found, first they looked at the bag with the old money in it. They each pulled out a few bills and spread them on the floor of the back porch. The money was wet, and it really smelled. However, they had to go through it and separate it.

The first thing they spotted was Benjamin Franklin's face, but it was smaller than on the bills that they had seen their parents carry.

"Do you guys realize," whispered Kevin, "that these are all one-hundred-dollar bills?"

"These must be older bills," said Dell. "Look at the face. It is much smaller than the bills of today."

"This is a lot of money," said Richie.

They pulled out more and some were beyond repair; others were barely recognizable. They made three piles: one pile with all good bills, another pile with bills that are missing the face or serial numbers, and the third pile was for all the destroyed bills. The boys did this for what seemed like hours. They had to be careful because the money was wet it could tear very easily, and they were trying to preserve as many as they could.

"I wonder how long we are going to be doing this. I am getting tired," said Richie.

It took them three hours to separate the piles of money.

While sorting, they came across money bands from the National Trust Bank of Wyoming.

This only proved their suspicion that this was the stolen money.

"I knew it. I knew this had to be the money from the robberies. There is entirely too much here for it not to be," said Kevin.

They still had to finish the puzzle of who this man was. Once the money was sorted, Dell decided that the damaged money be put in a trash bag but not thrown away. The boys agreed that this was a good idea.

All three boys collected the pile with the missing faces or serial numbers and put them in a separate bag.

Kevin said, "I can't believe it, all this money hidden for years in this town."

The boys began to count the good stack of money, and that took them another three hours to do. It was beginning to get dark outside when the boys finished counting their stacks. Richie ran into the house to find something to bind the stacks together, and all he could find was some of his mother's sewing lace. He gave some to each boy to bind their stacks as they were counting. After they got through counting and binding their stacks, they each gave their totals to Dell to add up. When he finished adding, he looked up and smiled the biggest smile that the boys had ever seen.

Dell cleared his throat and said, "Gentlemen, we have counted a total of $493,000."

Richie and Kevin could not believe their ears, nor could they believe that Old Man Harlow had not spent all of the stolen money.

Suddenly they heard Mrs. Ruiz coming down the hall to the back door. They quickly put the money into a third bag and pushed it under a chair, out of sight on the porch.

"Hey boys, your parents want you home for dinner," said Mrs. Ruiz.

They all bade each other farewell till tomorrow, grabbed their empty backpacks and bikes, and began to ride off.

"Hey guys, I need the walkie-talkies to recharge them for tomorrow in case we go back," said Dell.

Richie waved to them as they left, and then his mom turned to him with a sly smile and said, "What are you boys up to?"

"Nothing," Richie said with a little smile.

As she went back into the house, he waited until she had turned to go into the kitchen; he looked around at the mess on the floor then to the bags under the chair.

"Where can I hide the money?" he said.

Since nobody uses the back porch anymore, it became the storage area of the house. He spotted an old chair with an ottoman footstool. Richie went over to the footstool and found that the top came off exposing an inner hollow shell, a perfect spot to store the money.

"Please let no one find this," said Richie as he placed the ottoman lid on top of the footstool. He placed an old flower pot on top and piled up pillows around it to help hide it away from prying eyes.

He went into the house and washed his hands and almost forgot his backpack on the porch, which contained the letters, necklace, and baby rattle. He ran out there and grabbed the backpack and took it to his bedroom, and then he went down to eat dinner.

He walked into the kitchen and smelled the one thing he loved next to his parents and friends.

"Mom, did you make my favorite, mac 'n' cheese; you must really love me," Richie gushed to his mom.

"You know it, my boy." Mrs. Ruiz smiled.

That night, as each boy got ready for bed, they kept thinking about today's activities. The plan to get in and find something brilliant and to get out without being caught was genius. It had been a very stressful but an adventurous day, and they were all very tired and went straight to sleep. Their parents were in shock, because normally their sons stayed up past midnight during summer vacation. They assumed that riding all day and playing had really tired them out. If the parents knew the real reason behind their children's exhaustion, then their master plan would come to an end.

Beep, beep, beep! The alarm sounded, and each boy opened their eyes to a wet and rainy Saturday morning. Although they were in separate houses, they all awoke at the same time, 6:30 a.m.

"Ah man, we can't go to the old house in the rain," said Kevin as he was getting dressed.

He left his mom and dad a note to tell them that he had gone over to Richie's to hang out. As he was biking over to Richie's, he met up with Dell leaving his house with a piece of toast in his mouth.

"Off to Richie's?" he asked Kevin while chewing his toast.

Kevin nodded, and they both began to ride over the two blocks to Richie's house.

They both knocked on the door, and Mrs. Ruiz answered looking like she was still half asleep.

"What are you two doing here so early?" she said.

The two looked at each other and said, "We are here to play with Richie."

"At seven thirty in the morning?" she replied, looking somewhat suspicious at them. She let them in and pointed to the stairs. "Try and keep it down because I am going back to bed."

The boys said, "Yes, ma'am," and went upstairs to Richie's room. As they knocked then opened Richie's bedroom door, they found him fully dressed sitting on his bed playing a handheld basketball video game.

The other two jumped on his bed, startling him back to reality, and said, "Let's open the letters."

Richie put down the game and reached under his bed and pulled out the bag that held the letters, necklace, and baby rattle. The boys first examined the burnt letter. It was written on an old stationery paper with a floral design. The letter had yellowed with age and had creased lines as if it had been read again and again.

They spread it out carefully on Richie's desk; some parts of the letter were unreadable while they made out what they could.

> Jacob Wilcox Sr.
> Sheriff of Penskee, Wyoming
>
> My name is Harlow McK...
>
> 1951, 1952, ..., 1954, 1955 in these years...
> ...robbed National Trust Bank...
> I was going through a rough time and I...
> Totaling approx... $750,000.00....
> ...spent $75,000.00 of it.
> I hid some in a secret...son.
> I hid money in the house for you to find. Why make your job easy?
> ...am so sorry for this embarrassment for my family.
>
> Harlow McKenzie (Dec. 1970)
>
> Please forgive me.

The boys looked up after reading what they could and said, "Wow."

"This is his confession letter to the police, and he left some money for his son but didn't tell him where," Dell said.

"Do you think he knew that his son was a criminal as well?" asked Kevin.

"I don't know," said Richie, "but I guess he would have had to know that he was. This letter was written in 1970."

"He must not have liked his son enough to tell him where he hid it," said Kevin.

"Yeah, and the part about how he hid the money in the house for him to find, he didn't want to make his job easier. Who was he talking to, his son or the police?" said Dell.

"Well," said Richie, "we have kind of put a dent in the son's game by taking the money and finding this letter and the other stuff."

Dell and Kevin nodded their heads in agreement.

"Since we have read that letter, might as well read the other one now," Richie continued.

As Richie picked up the closed envelope, it felt a little heavy to him. The envelope had a bit of yellowing around the edges as if it had been in that stair compartment for a long time. When he unsealed the envelope, a large and heavy brass key fell onto the desk with a loud clang. The key looked very old; the top was shaped like a diamond. It had the name WB Safes stamped on each angle of the diamond.

"So there is a safe in the house," said Dell.

"Well, boys, we know that there must be some type of safe in the basement," said Kevin.

Richie nodded his head as he pulled the letter out of the envelope. They spread the letter out on his desk, and it was all written using block lettering just like the burnt letter. This letter too was written on floral stationery, and the paper was also yellowed with age. The writer had a really neat and steady hand while writing.

The boys all read the letter together taking turns reading each sentence aloud.

1969

To my son,

I know that I was not a great father to you, but I didn't mean for you to become like me, Alex, a criminal. I first heard about you while reading *The Trident* in 1969. You were 19 and had been arrested for breaking and entering, burglary, and other petty crimes. I was heartbroken that I was unable to be a role model for you. After your mom and I divorced in 1950, you were born. My life turned to crime because I didn't know any better, but I didn't want that life for you. I thought with me being out of your life that you would choose a different path than the one that I took. However, you did not, and that is partially my fault, and for that I am sorry, my son, that I was not there to guide and steer you in the right direction. I wrote this letter to tell you that I never stopped loving you, but I just could not mail it. If this letter is found by you, just know that my thoughts and prayers have always been with you.

Your loving dad,
Harlow McKenzie

P.S. The enclosed key opens a secret panel in the basement. I hope this will give you a fresh start.

The boys felt very sad for Old Man Harlow, and even though he robbed banks, he was not quite the bad guy that they had imagined!

"What do we do now?" asked Kevin.

"We go in the basement and find that secret panel and see what is behind it, and then we go to the police," said Dell.

"What's on the necklace and baby rattle?" asked Kevin.

Richie picked up the solid heart-shaped necklace and turned it over and read, "To my darling wife, Sasha... Love, Harlow."

The baby rattle had a similar inscription on the back as well; it read, "To my son Alex, may time heal all wounds... Love, Dad."

Now the boys knew that the necklace belonged to Old Man Harlow's wife, and the baby rattle was a gift to his son.

It was still early, and they wondered if they should chance a visit to the old house. As they looked outside it was still raining, but the sun was coming through, and the rain was turning into a light sprinkle. They decided to give the rain another hour to clear up, so they went downstairs and ate breakfast. They each had a bowl of Cocoa Puffs and loved the chocolaty milk in the bowl after the cereal was gone.

After breakfast, the boys went back upstairs to gather the letters, jewelry, and the key and waited for the rain to end. It sprinkled for another two hours. It was now noon, and they were getting restless and sick of watching TV. They went to go and sit on the front porch, when they saw the old '57 Chevy driving by with the son inside; he also had a passenger with him.

The boys wondered who could be in the truck with the son. Could it be someone to help him search the house? Was he giving a stranger a lift into town? It was now or never for the boys to get into that secret room in the basement.

CHAPTER 10

The Basement

After another hour, the rain stopped and the sun came out shining, bringing with it the hot mugginess of summertime rain. The boys packed a backpack with the walkie-talkies and the plastic bag with the letters, jewelry, and key. They also packed the sets of blueprints, two garbage bags, some small plastic bags, some granola bars, flashlights, and three bottled waters. They told Mrs. Ruiz that they were going riding and would be back by 7:00 p.m., if not sooner.

She yelled, "Be careful, boys, the rain might start up again."

They waved bye to her as they sped off toward the old house.

When they arrived at the house, they rode past the house and saw that the old '57 Chevy truck was parked in front. They heard all kinds of sounds coming from the house, banging, hammering, yelling, and the sound of drills.

Dell said, "He really wants that money, doesn't he?"

The other two just looked at him with small smiles on their faces. As they pulled up to the old textile factory across the street from the house, they parked their bikes inside like they had done previously. Since each boy had a backpack with stuff in it, they decided to go through their supplies once again and to take only what is necessary in the house this time. The boys had decided on the same plan as before: Kevin would follow the truck, and Richie and Dell would investigate the basement.

Dell handed out the walkie-talkies to each boy and told them that they were fully charged this time.

Kevin suggested, "Leave the backpack with all the stuff we found in the factory and take only the walkie-talkies, bags, flashlight, granola bars, water, and the key."

Dell liked this plan a lot. He said, "Why drag a bunch of stuff we don't really need this time?"

"Okay, okay," said Richie.

Both Richie and Dell each took a backpack and divided up their supplies. In Richie's backpack he put water, a granola bar, the key, and an empty bag. In Dell's backpack he took water, a granola bar, the walkie-talkie, flashlight, and an empty bag for whatever they might find.

"If by some chance," Richie told Kevin, "we get into trouble, you are to go straight to the sheriff and tell him everything. Take him to where the money is in the ottoman on the back porch." He continued, "That should be proof enough to get the sheriff to help us just in case something happens."

Kevin looked scared and so did the other two, but they knew they needed to do this in order to solve the rest of the mystery surrounding the old house. While the boys sat around the table in the factory taking turns looking out the window at the old house, suddenly the front door crashed open and the son came outside yelling and looking really angry. He jumped in his truck, started it, and sped off. Kevin jumped on his bike and said, "Off we go."

Dell called after him, "Channel 5, remember channel 5 for the walkie-talkies."

Kevin threw up his hand to let him know that he understood.

Dell and Richie ran across the gravel road and crept up the stairs to the front door. It was wide open, and the boys peeked in and heard nothing.

They entered and went for the doors along the right-hand side of the living room. The first door led to the kitchen. They tried the next door. It opened into a very large bathroom, and on the final try they opened the basement door. It was dark as they closed the door quietly behind them and began to go down the rickety staircase.

With every step they made, it creaked and creaked and creaked some more. It seemed like they would never get to the bottom of that staircase. When they came to the bottom, they waited until their eyes adjusted somewhat to the darkness, then they felt the garbage bags that Kevin that had fell on when he was in the basement. What he said was true: the smell was absolutely sickening. Then Dell remembered the flashlight and took it out of his backpack and turned it on.

Richie said, "Thanks, we needed that."

Dell just nodded. He was so scared, and Richie saw it in his eyes. He reached for Dell's hand and gave it a squeeze. Dell looked at Richie and smiled, for he felt that he could be brave with his best buddy there with him.

They began to shine the light around the basement and look at each wall, but it was still so dark in there that the light was only doing so much. They would have to get closer to the walls to touch them. The boys had to feel for some type of notch, keyhole, or lever. They were searching the east wall when they thought they heard a noise, so they stopped and listened really hard.

The boys looked at each other, shrugged their shoulders, and kept on searching the wall. They went to the south wall and searched—still nothing. Before they could search the west wall, they had to move old piles of newspapers and magazines from in front of it. It was minutes of exhausting labor, and the papers were all soggy and damp and smelled like something had died down there. Then the boys heard something slide across the floor above their heads. They knew they heard something this time, so they stopped moving the papers and listened.

They heard the scraping sound again, and then Dell pulled out the walkie-talkie and turned down the volume and pushed the button and whispered to Kevin, "Are you still following the son?"

Kevin said, "Yes, and he is all the way on the other side of town. He came to the Home Depot home center. By the looks of it, he is going to be in there for a while. I am outside but can see that he is walking back and forth with a shopping cart. I will radio back when he leaves, okay?" said Kevin.

Dell whispered, "Thanks for the information, but we think someone is in the house, right above us! We keep hearing furniture or something sliding around up there. We are still looking, but wanted you to know just in case you need to go the sheriff like we planned, okay?"

"No problem, and be careful," said Kevin.

As Dell was turning his walkie-talkie to a lower setting, it let out a loud beep, and both he and Richie froze. There was running footsteps overhead, and the basement door was thrown open and a head was looking down into the darkness. Richie and Dell were hiding behind the last stacks of newspapers, on the south wall.

Richie noticed the flashlight was still on pointed toward the floor. They were breathless. He grabbed Dell's hand and found the button on the flashlight to turn it off. Dell figured out what he was trying to do and pushed the off button very gently, as to not make any noise.

By this time both boys were shaking so hard that their knees were literally knocking against each other. Richie put his hand on Dell's shoulder to calm him down.

The strange man started coming down the stairs, then he would stop and listen. He did this for every other step. He heard nothing. Just when he got to the bottom step, a phone rang from the upper floor. He turned, went up the stairs, and closed and locked the door behind him.

Dell and Richie looked at one another and realized they were trapped! They looked around and saw the window and knew they couldn't get out through it; they were too big. They calmed down and got back to looking at the south wall after they had removed all of the papers. They searched it and nothing yet again. They had to keep searching until they figured out a plan to get out and to keep their minds from being trapped in a dark, damp, and smelly basement. The boys went over to the west wall and continued looking for anything that looked like a keyhole or a hole that a key could fit into. Again, nothing—absolutely nothing.

Richie said, "It has to be this north wall or nothing."

Dell looked at him and said sarcastically, "Umm, I would think so, being that it is the only one left."

Richie thought to himself, *Dell sure can be grouchy when he is scared*, but he didn't voice his opinion, for he was as scared as Dell, maybe even more. They continued looking until Dell's finger came across a hole halfway up the center of the wall. He punched Richie in the shoulder to let him know that he had found something.

Richie silently mouthed, "Ow."

Dell told Richie to get the key, and as he did, they heard the same sound from upstairs again. Somebody was moving furniture and hacking at the floor. They could feel the dust from the ceiling rain down on them.

Richie took the key from the backpack and placed it in the hole and began to turn it. The lock made a loud clicking-type sound like the sound a safe makes when you are opening it. With the last click, the entire panel swung open, knocking both boys onto the filthy damp floor. When they got up off the floor, they looked inside and was amazed to see stacks upon stacks of one hundred dollar bills, some pictures, cards, letters, and other little trinkets.

The boys packed everything into their two backpacks they were bulging. They closed the panel and tried to figure out a way to get out of the room. Dell went up the stairs and tried the door. He slowly turned the knob, but it was locked.

He tiptoed back down and whispered in a high-pitched voice, "We are stuck down here, and nobody knows we are here. What are we going to do?"

Dell began to panic, so Richie grabbed his arm and told him, "Calm it down and help me think of something!"

The boys looked at the window and said, "Let's try that way again."

Dell was first to try, but he got stuck and Richie had to pull him back in. When he did, he knocked over some glass bowls that were on the shelf next to the window. They paused, thinking that the person upstairs heard the sounds of the bowls crashing. But the boys heard no movement from above and they let out a sigh of relief.

"We have to hide the backpacks, Dell, in case someone finds us," said Richie.

Dell said, "Okay. Outside the window, I saw a little area that I can possibly reach to put them and throw something over them."

Richie said, "Okay, fine, hurry."

Dell again climbed halfway out the window, and Richie handed him his backpack. Dell tossed it to the side of the window and began to cover it with old rags lying there. Richie then handed him the other backpack, and Dell took out the granola bars and water and one walkie-talkie, just in case.

He then covered his backpack with some more rags that were littering the ground. Dell took one last look at the backpacks and couldn't tell that they were there; that was a good thing. Richie began pulling him back inside, and they both closed the window.

Richie asked, "Did you cover them well?"

Dell answered, "No one will know that they are there. Let's radio Kevin quickly."

Richie whispered into the walkie-talkie, "Kevin, Kevin, come in."

As they were trying to get Kevin, they heard running upstairs.

Kevin answered, "Is everything all right?"

Richie was talking very fast, "We are trapped. The backpacks are outside the basement window under some rags. Get them, okay?"

When he had finished talking to Kevin, a man threw open the basement door, saw them standing there, and said, "I knew someone was down here snooping around. Get over here."

He snatched the walkie-talkie from Richie and looked at it with a frown.

"Who were you talking to? Was it the sheriff?" asked the strange man. Then he threw the walkie-talkie on the ground and crushed it with his foot.

"Now," he said with an ugly sneer, "no one will ever know that you were down here snooping on us."

The boys prayed that Kevin had heard the man. Before the man snatched the walkie-talkie, Richie was holding down the button, to speak, so hopefully all was heard. Now their fates were in the hands of Kevin.

CHAPTER 11

Prisoners

"Who are you?" asked the big burly man.

The boys said nothing.

"I said, who are you, and what are you two doing here?" said the man.

The boys just stood there looking at him, for they didn't know what to tell him or if they should just be quiet; they were scared.

"Well, if you don't talk to me, then I will just have to get someone who you will talk to," sneered the man.

Dell went to open his mouth, and Richie stepped on his foot, to make him be quiet.

The man told them to get up the stairs. When the boys got through the basement door into the living room, the floors and the walls had more holes in them than when they entered the basement. They both saw the front door was open and made a run for it, but the man captured them by their collars and pulled them back in and threw them on the sofa. He then closed the front door and went to use his cell phone in the kitchen. Ritchie got up to try the door again, but the man had used a chain lock that he couldn't reach.

He looked at Dell while grabbing his hands and said, "I guess we are prisoners now, Dell, but don't worry. Kevin heard us and he will get help."

Dell just nodded his head and turned away so Richie wouldn't see the tear on his cheek.

*****

Kevin was frantic. He didn't know if he should go straight to the sheriff's or go to the old house.

"Oh no! Oh no!" Kevin said while shaking his head.

He was still outside Home Depot debating with himself when he saw the son come out yelling into his cell phone. Kevin figured that he was talking to the man at the old house. Now he knew that he had to follow him back to the house and try to rescue his friends. As the son sped off toward his house, Kevin took a shortcut through the woods and came out on the back side of the house near the lake.

He parked his bike behind the tool shed and crept around to the window and began to uncover the backpacks. He ran around to the back of the house with the backpacks and got on his bike and took off for Richie's house, which was three blocks away. It was his plan to hide the backpacks on the back porch then go back to see if he could get Dell and Richie out. It was 3:00 p.m.; he decided if he didn't get them out before 6:30 p.m. then he would go to the sheriff and tell him everything.

*****

The boys sat shaking with fear on the sofa as the man came back into the room.

He yelled, "You're going to be sorry, for you picked the wrong house to go snooping in."

"We weren't snooping," mumbled Richie under his breath.

Richie then asked if he could go to the bathroom. Before the man could answer, Dell asked if he could go.

The man said, "Okay, but both of you make it snappy."

The bathroom was directly across from where they were sitting. As they entered it, they were going to shut the door, when the man yelled to leave it open, and they did. Richie put his finger up to his mouth and motioned for Dell to use the bathroom, while he looked around it for some type of weapon. As Dell used the bathroom, Richie found a long flat-head screwdriver and a box cutter. He put them into his pants pocket, and he felt the key.

He didn't put the key in the backpack; he had forgotten. Richie could have kicked himself for forgetting this tiny thing.

Richie didn't want the son to find it, so he put the key into the bottom of his shoe. The man yelled it was time for them to come out and they did. He told them to get comfy on the sofa, for his friend was on his way and he wanted to meet them.

Kevin pedaled as fast as he could back to the old house, when he spotted the '57 Chevy rounding the corner. Kevin was closer to the factory door's entrance, so he rode his bike into the door as fast as he could and jumped off it as it kept rolling into the wall. He went to the window and peeked out and saw the son bring his truck to a screeching stop directly in front of the old house. He got out and ran to the door. The man in the house opened the door and began to talk to the son and was pointing at something inside.

The two men went further into the doorway, and they had their backs turned to the road, so Kevin thought that it was now or never. He ran for it as fast as he could across the gravel road. The sounds of the gravel under his foot were deafening he just knew that the two men would turn around and catch him. But they didn't; they just stood in the doorway talking very loud and fast. Kevin hid behind the wood pile and tried to listen, but all he could make out was "found them in the basement."

Kevin gasped loudly and covered his mouth, hoping no one heard.

When the son came into the house, anger was written all over his face, and he immediately began to question the two boys.

The son asked, "Who are you? What are you doing here? Have you been watching me? Does anybody know that you are here?"

"Answer me. I said answer me or so help me, I will make you wish you had never come into this house," said the son in a menacing voice.

Dell answered by saying, "We were just out exploring, and we saw this house and the side basement window was open, so we went in."

Richie cut in, "We didn't want anything. We were just playing around down there, like we were treasure hunters, that's all—honest."

Dell even started to cry while Richie continued the story. Richie thought he deserved an award for his acting abilities, but Richie played along and started to cry with him, even though he was not one to cry on the spur of the moment.

He began to rub his eyes and sniffle and said, "We tried to get out, but we got stuck, so we knocked a bowl over and that is when you came down and saw us."

The men went into the corner to talk this "story" over, and they began to argue. The other man, whose name was Jake, according to the son, shouted, "I want to keep them captive until we are finished," but the son wanted to let them go so they could finish without having to babysit some nosy brats.

He wanted to let them go so that they could continue looking for the loot, as Jake said rather loudly. Richie touched Dell's foot when he said this, and Dell nodded to let him know that he had heard it also. They were still crying, although no tears were coming out, and this was driving both men angrier. The men looked over at the boys and told them to quit their baby-crying or else. The boys stopped crying and began listening to their conversation.

Jake said, "Should we keep them here until we are done, or should we release them, Alex? Make up your mind."

For the first time, the boys had heard the son's name; it was Alex, the same name that was on the baby rattle. They knew they had discovered the identity of Old Man's Harlow son, if only they would live to tell someone.

Alex said, "We could always throw them back in the basement, because we still needed to search the attic and the other bedrooms."

"Yeah, let's do that, toss them back down there because they can't get out. The boy said that they got stuck, so we know where they will be," Jake said with a chuckle.

Alex said, "We have to hurry because people are becoming suspicious in town, asking a lot of questions every time I go in to buy a new tool or something. I am getting really tired of this boring town anyways."

Jake said, "I can't believe your father ever lived in such a dreary place. If he did rob those banks, why stay here, why not move away? I just don't get it."

"When I found this old deed in my mother's bank deposit box, I almost flipped. I had found all sorts of news clippings about the robberies and that my old man was believed to be the suspect in them. The last clipping nearly made me choke on my gum I was chewing. It told of how the amounts of the robberies were nearly one million dollars. That the cops didn't find it, but they always suspected him and believed him to be in possession of the money," said Alex with a sly grin.

Alex could remember the clippings as if it was yesterday. It had been five years ago before he had gone to prison for the fifteenth time for petty theft. That is where he met Jake Bryant. He was in prison for breaking and entering, and they both had a two-year sentence. Alex got out early for good behavior, while Jake served his entire two-year sentence, because he got into some fights while serving his time.

As soon as Alex got out, he planned to come to Wyoming and find this small town and search this house for the missing money. When he ran into problems looking for the money, he wrote a letter to Jake to come help him, and he would split the money with him. Jake wrote back that he would be there, and within a week's time, he joined Alex in searching for the money. Now they were both in the living room deciding what to do with a couple of nosy kids who were playing in their house.

Jake said, "Let's throw them back in the basement for now and we can decide later after we search the attic."

Alex nodded his head in approval and told the boys to get up and get back over to the basement door. As the boys got to the door, Jake opened the door and pushed the boys down the stairs and locked the door behind them. The boys stumbled down a few steps but didn't lose their footing. They heard the men going up the stairs to the attic, and the boys breathed a sigh of relief.

"Now we have to get out of here," said Dell, "before they come back to get us."

CHAPTER 12

The Escape

Outside Kevin was watching this whole scene play out before his eyes. He was rooted to the spot on the porch looking in through one of the bay windows that were missing a small bit of newspaper. He saw the boys crying and the men telling them to be quiet. Kevin just knew something bad was going to happen. He was about to go for help when he saw the man push them into the basement. He tiptoed off the porch, jumped down to the ground, crawled around to the basement window, and began calling their names in a whisper.

"Dell, Richie, are you there? It's me, Kevin," he whispered.

Both boys ran over to the window, and Kevin grabbed both of their hands and whispered, "You both have to get out now."

Dell tried to get out through the window and couldn't. Richie tried, and he too couldn't fit. Kevin looked around to see if there were any other window in the basement, and he didn't see any on the side where they were. He went to the back of the house and he found another window; it looked bigger.

Kevin ran back around to the open window and said, "Hold on guys, I found another window. It looks bigger. I need to move the stuff blocking it."

The other two boys smiled with relief. They were going to get out, hopefully.

There were old tires and wood pieces covering the window, so as quietly as he could, he began to remove the tires, first one, and then another after five tires. He started on the wood pieces until the window was clear. Richie and Dell noticed light was coming from the wall that they had moved the newspapers to, so they began to move the newspapers once again back in front of where the secret panel was. As they moved the paper, they saw Kevin's legs and thought, *That window does look bigger. Maybe we can get out.* With more light in the basement, they saw that there was an old floor model TV directly under the window.

Dell went over the window and found that it was painted shut and said, "How are we going to get the paint off? It is really thick it has sealed the window."

He remembered the screwdriver and the box cutter Richie took from the upstairs bathroom.

Dell told Richie, "Give me the screwdriver and you take the box cutter and start scraping the paint off, okay?"

Richie nodded and said, "Good thinking, Dell."

Richie then remembered the bottled water that Dell had taken out of the backpacks and went to look for them. When he found them, he began to splash the water around the window to soften the paint as they scraped.

The water made it easier to scrape off the paint and pry the window open. Kevin was holding the window open from the outside so the boys could climb through. It was a tight fit, but both managed to get out and lower the window without make a sound.

They crept back around the side of the house and heard the banging of the axes on the walls in the attic. The boys ran across the gravel road into the factory and sat down.

Then Dell stood up and cried, "Oh no, we forgot our backpacks."

He started to go back out the door, when Kevin grabbed him and said, "I already got them and took them to Richie's house."

Richie and Dell gave Kevin high fives as they got on their bikes. They told him they thought that he was an awesome dude for coming back to rescue them. They peeked out the window to make sure the way was clear, and then they took off for home. As they were riding home, they decided that it was time to go to the police and tell them the whole story. By now it was too late, and they were tired from today's quest, so they decided to go to the sheriff on Monday.

They decided Monday because their parents always had them doing stuff on Sunday like going to church, yard work, and just general cleaning duties before the next week began. The boys knew that Sunday was not the day to turn in both Alex and Jake, but Monday would be the day when this would all come to an end. They hoped to spend the last two weeks of their summer vacation on the lake fishing.

First, they had to go through their backpacks and arrange all the evidence for the sheriff. That would take the rest of the evening to do. The boys decided to have a sleepover at Dell's house, and all they had to do was transport the money and everything else to Dell's house because he lived closest to the sheriff's station. The boys figured that they could walk it all over on Monday morning.

When the boys arrived at Richie's house, it was around 6:00 p.m., and they were filthy and smelled like they had been playing in a trash bin. Mrs. Ruiz wondered how boys could get so dirty just riding their bikes, but she shook her head and asked them if they wanted to eat dinner. The boys looked at one another, and with exhausted sighs, "Yes, we would love dinner."

She had them all go into the bathroom and clean up as best they could, at least to get rid of some of that sweaty stench. Mrs. Ruiz made them chicken strips, mashed potatoes, and corn on the cob. She had Dell and Kevin call their parents to let them know that they were eating dinner here tonight. While Dell was talking to his dad, he asked if he could have a sleepover at the house tonight. His dad said, "No problem." Kevin too asked his parents if he could camp over at Dell's tonight, and his mom told him, "Sure you could, and you are to behave yourself and be polite."

Kevin told his mom, "Come on, you know I am a little angel. I will be the best child ever."

She said, "Uh-huh, yeah, have fun."

While they were eating their dinner, Richie asked his mom about sleeping over at Dell's, and she nodded yes. However, she told him to take a shower before going to bed, then turned to all the boys and said, "All of you take a shower before going to bed. You smell really bad. I don't think Mrs. McPhearson will appreciate the stench coming from Dell's room if you don't." She giggled as she turned and went back into the kitchen to clean up.

After dinner, Richie went up to his room and packed his overnight bag and met Dell and Kevin outside with their bikes and all of their backpacks, stuffed to the brim. Richie had to go to the back porch to get the money bags. He put those three bags into another duffel bag to disguise it. They could barely carry all the bags they had. They were so heavy, and they had to make a stop at Kevin's before they had to bike over to Dell's. This was going to be interesting. They stopped at Kevin's house to get his overnight bag. When they pulled up to Kevin's house, Mr. McNeal was outside washing his truck. He asked the boys if they wanted a ride to Dell's, since they were carrying so much stuff.

They said, "Yes, and thank you very much."

Kevin added, "Dad, you're the best." He began to load up the boys' bicycles, backpacks, and Richie's overnight bag.

Mr. McNeal asked, "What is in all of these backpacks and this duffel bag? They are quite heavy."

The boys shuffled their feet and said it's just stuff they found while out riding their bikes. He gave them a funny look, and at that moment, before he could ask anything else, Kevin came running out of the house with his overnight bag. He threw it into the back with everything else and they climbed into the truck, put their seatbelts on, and they were off to Dell's house.

As they were driving over to Dell's, they spotted the '57 Chevy in front of them. The boys kind of ducked down in their seats as if they were looking for something on the floor, so they wouldn't be suspicious to Kevin's dad. The '57 Chevy truck suddenly turned to the right. They were heading to the grocery store on the corner, and the boys let out a long breath of relief. Mr. McNeal and the boys pulled up at Dell's at 8:00 p.m. The ride had taken less than ten minutes.

Mr. McNeal took out their bikes from the back of his truck, while the boys were unloading all of their bags and backpacks in Dell's garage. As soon as Kevin's dad was done unloading the bikes, each boy thanked him, and they took their bikes into the garage. Mr. McPhearson came out to greet Mr. McNeal, and they talked for a few minutes, then he hopped in his truck, waved at the boys, and took off back home.

Mr. McPhearson told them that he was going to lock the garage from the outside.

"When you are ready, come in the house. Just go through the garage door that leads into the house," said Dell's dad.

The boys all nodded their heads as he left them alone in the spacious garage. They immediately went to the two backpacks that held what they had found in the basement today. In the first was the money; it was in great condition, as if they had gone to the bank and got it that day. They locked the door to the garage and then started counting; it was exactly one hundred fifty thousand dollars.

"This is the secret money that Old Man Harlow wanted to give to his son so that he could start a new life," said Richie.

In the other, they examined the cards, letters, photo album, and the trinkets that were in the secret safe. The cards were old birthday cards and cards that seem to be still sealed, but were never mailed to his son and wife. The letters were old love letters between Old Man Harlow and his wife, Sasha. It seems they were written before they were married, but the boys couldn't tell, because they were not dated. The trinkets were just old rings, watches, and cuff links; some looked to be very old, possibly family heirlooms.

The photo album had pictures of a man and woman on the lake, having a picnic; there were different poses. Also, there was some of a little boy in different poses, probably school pictures. There were what looked like pictures of different cars and people posing by them and by the very house that they were in today. It was a very old photo album, and it looked as if Old Man Harlow really treasured this album because he kept it in a place where it couldn't get ruined by the elements. Unlike the money he hid in the attic, these things in the safe he really cared about.

The boys had finally figured out the story of Old Man Harlow and his son. As the boys hid their stuff in an old trash can at the back of the garage. They felt relieved that it was all over and that they had survived to tell their story. They locked the garage and went upstairs to Dell's room. They each took a much-needed shower and went to bed knowing that this adventure was coming to an end. Now all that was left was to take everything to the sheriff, and for the first time in two months, the boys slept with no worries that night.

CHAPTER 13

Going to the Sheriff

The boys awoke to a rainy Sunday morning, and all they could think about was the mystery of Old Man Harlow and his home were over. When they eventually got up, they were very quiet, and each boy just lay there thinking about the events of the past few days. When one of them finally spoke, it made the others jump, and they all started to laugh.

Dell said, "I am so glad that this is over. It was exciting, but I would rather fish any day."

"Well, I rather would have liked to play basketball all summer, but that's just me," chuckled Richie.

"If it was up to me, I would love this kind of excitement on a daily basis—if it were up to me," said Kevin in a most serious tone.

The other two looked at him and said almost at the same time, "Are you crazy?"

Kevin looked at them and started to laugh so hard he had to grab his sides to keep them from hurting. Once he started laughing, the other two joined in, and soon, they were wrestling all over the floor, acting like boys.

Mr. McPhearson was already awake and dressed as the boys came down for breakfast. They saw Mrs. McPhearson, and she greeted them all with a huge hug and a warm smile. For breakfast she made them pancakes, eggs, and sausages. With a full mouth, Dell said, "This is delicious, Mom!" Richie and Kevin followed with the same compliment with cheeks as full as chipmunks.

While the boys were getting ready for church, Mr. McPhearson was in the garage searching for a hammer and nails to hang a painting for his wife. In searching for the hammer, he looked behind things and under old tarps, when his eyes rested upon a hammer beside the garbage can where the boys had stored the items from the house. As he was reaching to pick it up, the tip of the hammer knocked the trash can lid off. When he went to put it back on, he spotted a backpack that had money sticking out. He unzipped the compartment and realized there were lots of dollars, and they were all hundred-dollar bills.

Mr. McPhearson began to panic and wondered what his son was mixed up in.

"That Dell, what is this all about? He had better have a good explanation, or so help me," said Mr. McPhearson.

He had let Dell borrow some walkie-talkies; maybe he used them to rob a bank with his friends, for Dell was quite clever for a boy of eleven.

"No, no, no," said Dell's dad, "my son would never do anything like that, nor would his friends."

Besides, they were children. How could children rob a bank? thought Mr. McPhearson, and he laughed to himself. He had to find out where this money came from, and he had to know now.

When Mr. McPhearson came back in the house with the hammer and no nails, he asked the boys to come in the garage and help him look for them. They agreed and followed him to the garage. They strolled into the garage and their eyes fell upon the trash can; the lid was missing.

Mr. McPhearson watched as the boys nervously began looking for the nails, for he knew they *knew* the trash can lid was off. All three boys kept throwing looks at each other while searching for the nails, until Dell's dad informed them that he had removed the lid. Dell dropped the box of nails he had just found and stood there looking at his dad with his mouth open.

"What exactly have you boys been up to while out riding this summer?" asked Mr. McPhearson.

The boys looked at one another, and Richie looked up and said, "It's a long story, and I guess we will start at the beginning."

The boys started telling Mr. McPhearson about the first time they went riding out on the gravel road, when they spotted someone going into one of the old houses. They went on to tell him the entire story, about the blueprint differences, the secret places in the house, the money, trinkets, and finally about the two men that were in the house.

"Yeah, Dad. Yesterday Richie and I became their prisoners, and Kevin rescued us from the basement, and we got away with all the evidence," concluded Dell.

Mr. McPhearson's mouth was open the entire time, looking from child to child to child. He was in disbelief at what these children went through and how close they came to being harmed by these two strange men. The boys and Mr. McPhearson never made it to church that Sunday. Mrs. McPhearson left them in the garage talking, while she went. The boys and Mr. McPhearson stayed home discussing the events that had brought them to this point, and they ended by telling Dell's dad that they were going to the sheriff in the morning and taking all the evidence with them. Mr. McPhearson offered to stay home from work and go with them for support. At that moment he looked at Dell and told him that he was very proud of him for acting like a very mature young man, even though he knew he was scared. He then hugged his son—he hugged them all.

However, he told them if they ever ran across something like this again, that they were to come straight to him and let him handle it. They were too young to deal with this type of adventure without some grown-up supervision. The boys just looked at each other and smiled, for they knew that they were much smarter than their parents gave them credit for. Mr. McPhearson informed the other two boys that he would be calling their parents and telling them the story as well. He would also be asking their parents if they could camp out one more night; he would bring them home tomorrow evening.

As the McNeals and the Ruizes came to Dell's house to bring fresh clothes for Monday, they all wanted to hear the story again and again. They asked many questions and couldn't believe that their children had solved a mystery this complex. The parents then kissed their kids goodnight and thanked Mr. McPhearson for going in with them tomorrow, and if he needed them for anything, all he had to do was call. He nodded and thanked them for coming over to support the boys.

After each boy's parents left, Mrs. McPhearson made them a light dinner of tuna sandwiches, pickles, chips, and carrot sticks with ranch. They all went to bed after dinner, and the boys went to sleep with thoughts of the sheriff handcuffing them and throwing them in jail. They didn't sleep well at all.

Monday morning, they all awoke to a bright and sunny day. They all felt refreshed despite the bad dreams of going to jail and never seeing their family again.

However, they got dressed and had breakfast. While they were eating, Mrs. McPhearson came into the kitchen and told the boys to be brave and that she was very proud of them. Then she was off to work. Dell's dad came down dressed; he had a cup of coffee while the boys finished their cereal. They all ate in silence, and then Mr. McPhearson told them they should leave about 9:30 a.m. He had already called the sheriff to inform him that the boys were coming in with some substantial information that they had uncovered.

While the boys packed everything to take to the sheriff's station, Mr. McPhearson helped them put it into the bed of his truck in one large tote. They all hopped into the truck and were off to tell their story once again. As they were driving to the sheriff's station, the boys saw the old '57 Chevy truck and pointed it out to Dell's dad, who wrote the license plate number down on a pad; it was 4LD25A—Illinois plate. He put the pad in his glove box for safekeeping.

When they pulled up to the station, the boys suddenly got nervous, and Dell said, "No one will believe us."

But Mr. McPhearson told them that it was fine for them to be nervous. They had nothing to worry about. They knew the truth, and they had evidence to back it up.

They greeted the sheriff at the door to the station while Mr. McPhearson was dragging the tote in behind them. As they were walking in, they spotted a bulletin board that had all the top ten criminals wanted and old flyers of missing people and children. Then one flyer jumped out at Kevin, who was reading it as he walked. He stopped so suddenly that Richie walked into him. Kevin pointed at the flyer, and the boys went to go and get a better look at it. It was an old yellowed and faded flyer from the 1950s, and it talked about the bank robberies of the National Trust Bank of Wyoming.

Kevin pulled it from the board and carried it into the sheriff's office behind Mr. McPhearson. The sheriff offered them all a seat and asked if they wanted something to drink. They all replied, "Yes."

Dell's dad said, "I'll take a coffee with sugar."

The boys all said together, "Fruit punch for us please."

The sheriff laughed and said, "Okay, one coffee and three fruit punches." He told his deputy to run to the store next door and get three fruit punch drinks, while he made Mr. McPhearson a cup of coffee.

"While we wait for your drinks, you can begin telling me what this visit is all about," said the sheriff.

Kevin put the flyer on his desk and told him it was about the bank robberies of the early 1950s.

"Bank robberies, well, my father was the sheriff during that time, and he had a suspect but no proof that the person had committed the crime." The sheriff continued, "The case became cold, and several deputies have worked to solve it over the last fifty years. However, they had never come up with anything that could be used against the suspected individual. Then in 1975 their suspect died, so the case remained officially open but cold."

The boys all looked at each other and then began taking turns telling the sheriff everything that they had done in the past two months. This took around three hours to explain, because of all the evidence the boys had, it had to be explained and tagged. Since this was a bank robbery, the crime fell under the jurisdiction of the federal government. So the sheriff called the FBI in to oversee the investigation, to see if anyone would be prosecuted for the crime.

After the FBI agent, Donald Barber, arrived, the boys had to explain once again what they had been up to during their summer vacation and again took another three hours. By the time they were finished, it was 4:30 p.m., their juices had been drunk a long time ago, and the deputy went back to the store and purchased three more with some snack cakes this time.

While the FBI was busy cataloging all the evidence from the sheriff's station, Special Agent Barber told the boys that there was a reward for any information about this case. The reward has never been revoked.

The boys said, "Reward, as in money?"

The agent laughed and said, "Yes, as in money, as in thirty thousand dollars.

"No way," said Richie.

"I'll believe it when I see it," said Kevin. "I'm going to buy me some new tennis shoes; mine got messed up in that nasty basement."

Special Agent Barber patted the boys on their backs and said, "The money is yours."

The boys screamed and hugged each other and gave out high fives to the deputies and the sheriff.

After they had settled down a bit, Sheriff Wilcox Jr. asked them, "When was the last time you guys seen Alex McKenzie and Jake Bryant?"

Dell answered, "Saturday afternoon, after they threw us back into the basement."

But then Richie said, "Well, we saw the truck this morning as we were coming to the station."

Sheriff Wilcox Jr. said, "I wish we had some way of tracking the truck so that we can put out an APB (all-points bulletin) for the vehicle."

Mr. McPhearson said, "I wrote down the license plate number after the boys told me about the truck. Let me go out and get it."

He rushed out and came back in with a slip of paper with the license plate number on it. The number was 4LD25A—Illinois plate. The FBI immediately put out an APB on a navy blue '57 Chevy truck with tinted windows. The sheriff's department also set up road checkpoints on all highways coming in and out of the town. They also issued warrants for Alex McKenzie and Jake Bryant for questioning.

Once again Sheriff Wilcox Jr. and Special Agent Barber thanked the boys for all their hard work. They told them in the future that they might want to get the authorities involved in the event of an emergency instead of trying to handle it themselves. "This could have turned out a lot worse for you boys if you had not used your heads." The boys said they will and took both the sheriff's and the FBI's business cards for future reference. They then left the station, and Dell's dad took them all for pizza and ice cream.

As the boys were enjoying their pizza, they began to talk of their new school year that was rapidly approaching.

Dell said, "I hope I am in Mr. Barratt's class because his class does a lot of outdoor activities, and I like to be outdoors."

"All I wish for is chicken nuggets in the cafeteria. We never get chicken nuggets. It makes me cry to walk into the lunchroom and they have fish sticks. I hate fish sticks," said Richie.

Mr. McPhearson laughed out loud almost choking on his pizza. He said, "In my time, all we wished for was the spaghetti and meatballs. It was delicious."

Kevin said, "All I want to do is play basketball for PE and nothing else. I think this year I am going to try out for the Junior Basketball League. I have been practicing with my dad, and he says I am pretty good."

The boys kept talking about other things as Mr. McPhearson sat there watching all three boys and gaining a new respect for them for what they had accomplished. He couldn't help but be proud. After they had finished their dinner, he brought them back to the house so that they could pick up their overnight bags. Mr. McPhearson took Kevin and Richie home, and Dell told them both he would call them in a couple of days.

CHAPTER 14

The Tale of Alex McKenzie

True to his word, Dell called each of his friends on Wednesday morning using three-way calling. They were all talking when Mr. McNeal came in to tell Kevin that he needs to get dressed because they all had to go down to the sheriff's station for a follow-up report. At the same time both Dell's and Richie's parents told them the same also. The boys said bye to each other and hung up the phone.

When the families arrived, they greeted each other and were taken into a conference room, where several men were seated.

Richie pulled Dell and Kevin by the collar and whispered, "They're going to arrest us. Should we make a break for the door before they grab us?"

Dell looked at him and said, "Did you eat Fruit Loops this morning? Because you sound a little loopy."

Kevin looked at them both and busted out in giggles and had to pretend he was coughing. He was laughing so hard.

Sheriff Wilcox Jr. got up and made the introductions. First he introduced the FBI agent in charge, Special Agent Barber. "This is the federal attorney that would be handling any charges being filed, Federal Prosecutor Patrick Anderson." There were also several reporters from different newspapers, including the local paper, *The Trident*, and finally, a very old man who was in a motorized wheelchair.

Sheriff Wilcox Jr. made this introduction special; as he was looking at the boys, he told them that this was his father, Sheriff Wilcox Sr. Their parents all nudged the boys to get up and go shake his hand, and they did with a smile on their faces.

The former sheriff thanked the boys for solving the case and finding the missing money. He went on to tell them that when he first got the case, he just knew that he would solve it. It had been harder than he thought. In all these years since retiring and watching his son take his place, he still never forgot the case.

He expressed his gratitude and said, "Never in a million years would I ever think that a nine-, ten-, and an eleven-year-old would have solved the case." As he was guiding his chair back to the table, he said with a chuckle, "Kids these days."

Everyone in the room laughed at this remark. Sheriff Wilcox Jr. told the group that they wanted to inform them of what had happened since their last visit on Monday.

"After we put out the APB on both men, it still took us about ten hours to locate them. They were heading out of town on Highway 80, going about ninety miles per hour. They were arrested and booked in our jail. Since this was a joint task between the Penskee Sheriff's Department and the FBI, we decided to split up the work. So the FBI took all the evidence that you boys collected and processed it, while we processed the house and questioned the two men," said Sheriff Wilcox Jr.

"When we arrived at the house, it was in a complete shamble—every wall was hacked into, every floorboard was pulled up, just as you boys described," stated the sheriff.

He continued, "They even went so far as to remove all the bathroom and kitchen appliances and fixtures. A few tools littered the floor on every level of the house. We also found rental receipts where they had rented jackhammers for the concrete basement, which they never got a chance to explore."

Sheriff Wilcox Jr. finished by saying, "It was a good thing you boys got to the areas of the house when you did, for with the supplies they had, they would have eventually found everything."

All the boys nodded in agreement with huge smiles on their faces.

Special Agent Barber took over by saying, "We didn't find any weapons in their possession; however, both men had outstanding warrants in Illinois for burglary. They will be sent back there to stand trial for those crimes, then will come back here to stand trial for breaking and entering and false imprisonment according to the Penskee county prosecutor, Maxwell Neely.

"In our research of Alex McKenzie, he was born in 1950 in Chicago, Illinois. He has had a long history in the criminal courts. It all started after his mother was diagnosed with breast cancer at the age of fourteen. He began breaking into neighbors' houses with his friends, because he had no home supervision. His mother was in and out of the hospital getting treated, and she didn't have the strength to really see after him. Alex basically raised himself. At the age of seventeen he stole his first car for a joyride and ended up in a fender bender. He then became prison bound at the age of nineteen, when he tried to rob a bank with a few of his friends. The plan went haywire when a bank employee spotted them putting on masks and the police were called. His friends got away, but he didn't—he paid the price for all of them."

Special Agent Barber continued, "Alex McKenzie went on to have a life of crime. He's been in and out of prison fifteen times. He never stayed in contact with his mother; she died from breast cancer complications while he was in prison in 1970. Three years ago was his last time in jail, and that is where he met Jake Bryant, his cellmate. Alex told Jake that when his mother died, she left a note telling him where her safe deposit box was. That was the legacy she left him, her safe deposit box. In that box was a letter from his mother, a letter from his dad that had been written at the time of his birth, and another letter that had been written to the sheriff but was sent to the ex-wife Sasha by mistake. There were also some newspaper clippings, jewelry, cash that totaled two thousand dollars, and a deed to the property at 3254 Beacon Road along with the key to the house."

"The burnt letter that you boys found in the trash pile was that very letter that was addressed to my dad," said Sheriff Wilcox Jr. He continued, "The letter that Old Man Harlow wrote him and sent to his wife was the very same letter you boys found in that false staircase. As we sit here talking, Alex and Jake are in a jail cell in Chicago, Illinois. They have both written confessions to all the crimes they have committed."

Special Agent Barber concluded by saying, "They confessed to all the burglaries in Chicago and the breaking and entering here in Penskee. They are fighting the false imprisonment charge because they said that the boys had trespassed on his property. Although the house was never left for Alex or put in his name, he felt the house was his since his father owned it."

Sheriff Wilcox Jr. said, "I don't think you boys will even have to show up in court to testify since they wrote a confession." With those words, the boys sighed a sound of relief, "Ah, good."

"We just called you all here to let you know that we are going to give you three boys the reward for finding the money. As we talked to your parents this morning, they have decided to start your college funds with a portion of the money and the rest is to be yours to do with as you please," said Special Agent Barber.

The boys looked at each other and said, "How much exactly is the reward?"

"The reward is exactly thirty thousand dollars, to be split three ways among you boys," said Special Agent Barber.

"Wow," said all three boys together.

"We thought you were playing on Monday when you talked about the reward," said Richie, laughing.

"As your parents knew you were getting this reward this morning, they decided that a portion of the money was going toward your college education; the rest will go into separate bank accounts where you will have access to the money whenever you wish," said Prosecutor Anderson.

He went on to finish explaining to the families about their reward.

The boys had an ingenious plan as to what to do with their own individual portion.

When Prosecutor Anderson was finished speaking to their parents, he turned to the boys and told them that their own personal bank accounts would be in the amount of two thousand dollars each.

He then told them, "In a few weeks they would get their own ATM card and a pin number, but they would have to come into the bank to take a photo ID for their ATM cards."

The boys were so excited they jumped up, grabbed each other, and danced around. Everybody in the room began to laugh and shake their hands. As the boys walked out, all the deputies stood and gave them a standing ovation. The boys were so pleased with themselves and what they had accomplished; they just couldn't wait to see what they would do with their monies.

CHAPTER 15

End of Summer Vacation

During the next week the boys were busy getting their pictures taken for the local newspaper, *The Trident*, and at the bank getting their photos taken for their new ATM cards. The story had gotten out all over town about these three boys who had found the missing money from those bank robberies in the early 1950s. Everyone in town always suspected Harlow McKenzie of the robberies, but they had no proof until now.

No one in town ever knew that he had a son and that his son also turned out to be a criminal. The people in the town of Penskee decided it was time to pay attention to their neighbors and to know what is going on so that this won't happen again in their small town. The whole town gathered together to throw the boys a barbeque for solving the fifty-year-old mystery that kept gossip alive in Penskee, Wyoming.

After all the celebrations, parades, and cookouts in their honor, their celebrity died down a bit. The boys had one week before the summer vacation was over and school would be starting once again. They felt as if they had no chance to relax all summer and just wanted this one week to do so. They still had not decided what to do with their money they had in the bank. Every time they began to discuss it, they would get frustrated because they couldn't come up with one thing to spend it on. The boys knew that they wanted to build a clubhouse but didn't know how to do it.

They figured they had six thousand dollars between them and that could build a very nice clubhouse, but where would they put it? Their own backyards were too small to house such a building, so they were stuck about what to do. Dell thought if they could find a piece of land that no one used then they could build it there, but how would they get a piece of land being only kids?

Then Kevin came up with a plan to start their own detective agency. "You know, to find missing pets and things like that."

They all thought that was a good idea, something they could do on the weekends to keep them out of trouble. However, they didn't know what it would take to run a detective agency, so they thought that they would go and ask the sheriff for some advice.

On Tuesday, they walked into the sheriff's office to see if they could talk to Sheriff Wilcox. He came out and told them his door is always open to them.

The boys began to ask him all sorts of information about a detective agency. They asked, "What kind of stuff would we need?" They really wanted to be professional about it. They asked him so many questions that he couldn't keep up with giving them the answers. After they had finished asking him everything they could think of, he sat back in his chair and folded his arms and looked at each boy.

"You guys are for real, aren't you?" he asked them.

They all said together, "Yes."

He was very impressed and told them that they needed to get a business license, someone to sponsor them, and a place that they could set up as a place of business. Then they would officially be detectives.

The boys said, "We can do that!"

Nevertheless, they still had to get a business license, sponsor, and find a place to have their agency. This was too stressful to think about, so the boys decided to go fishing and do or think about nothing.

While fishing, they began to talk yet again about their first case they had stumbled upon and how they had solved it all by themselves. The boys wondered about school and how they would handle it during schooltime, but they didn't let that change their mind about the detective agency. As Richie kept catching fish, the other two were playing swords with their poles, and after the twentieth fish that Richie had caught, they decided to go home. When they got to the fork in their road, they all went their separate ways and said they would meet again tomorrow to talk about their detective agency.

Richie opened the front door of his house, and both his mom and dad were waiting for him. He checked his watch and it was 5:30 p.m., so he knew he wasn't in trouble for being late. Then he thought he had forgotten to take out the trash this morning, but he looked out the window and the trash cans were in their spot, so he wasn't in trouble for that.

He smiled and showed his parents all the fish he had caught in his bucket. He knew that would cheer them up. They smiled, but his mom told him to put them in the kitchen then come back and sit down; they had to talk to him. He went to put the fish in the sink, then came back and sat down in front of them. He knew this would not be good news by the looks of their faces.

Mr. Ruiz leaned forward and told Richie in a most serious tone, "Hey bud, I got some good news. I got a promotion at my job, and with that we are going to be moving to a much bigger place."

Richie said, "Moving? Moving where? Not out of the town, not away from my friends! How could you do this to me? We are going to start our own detective agency."

His parents looked at one another and started to laugh first softly, then they began to hold their stomach, and all Richie could do was look back and forth at the both of them. He was still upset about having to move, to leave his friends, and to start fresh somewhere else. He hated the whole idea altogether.

Then his dad looked at him and said, "Yes, my boy, we are moving, but not out of the town, nor out of the state, but down the way off Beacon Road, down by the lake, in the new development on this side of Green River."

Richie stood up and said, "No way, down by Old Man Harlow's house?"

His dad let out another laugh and said, "Close but about a mile away on the other side of the lake."

"As a matter of fact, we will be living one block from Kevin's family and one block from Dell's family so you three will always live by one another," said Mr. Ruiz.

"We have been building the house in secret all summer, that is why all that stuff is out there on the back porch. It is time to clean and clear out what we are not taking to the new house. This house has been sold, and the new owners arrive in five weeks, so we have a lot of stuff to do, all right?"

"All right," said Richie.

"Can I go and call the guys to let them know the good news?" said Richie.

"Go ahead," said his mom.

"Dinner will be in an hour, all right?" said Mrs. Ruiz.

"All right, Mom," said Richie.

Richie went upstairs to his room and called the boys and told them the news. They were so excited. Now they can walk to school together and they can see each other from their backyards. That is going to be so awesome.

Richie said, "We are going to go and look at the house tomorrow so that I can tell you both what it looks like."

He then hung up with the boys and went down to dinner, and his mom had made one of his favorite dinners, sloppy joes and french fries. Richie went to bed that night a happy boy; and he dreamed of his new house, their detective agency, and of all things good.

Epilogue

Today was Thursday, only three more days of summer till Monday. Richie woke up early. He really wanted to go and see the house. He kept pacing back and forth in front of his parents' bedroom door, wanting to ask them more questions. He decided to go and take a shower and get dressed.

When he got out, his parents were still asleep. After getting dressed, he went downstairs and had breakfast. It was around 10:00 a.m. when his parents came down, and they were quite surprised to see Richie up, dressed, and waiting for them.

"I have been waiting for hours," said Richie.

"Really," said his dad, with a light chuckle.

Richie's parents decided to forget about breakfast, seeing that their little one was growing impatient. As they took off from their newly sold house, they decided to drive along the gravel road to get to their new home. Richie looked at Old Man Harlow's house and saw that there were a couple of bulldozers parked on the lawn. People were outside standing around tables looking at blueprints. Richie wondered what they were going to do to the house.

As they pulled up to their brand-new house, it was still under construction but was almost completed. The driveway, which was a three-car garage driveway, was filled with trucks that had signs on the door like, Contractor, Electrical, Water, Gas, and a host of others; they had to park on the street. The house was twice the size of their old house. Richie was in awe he couldn't even speak. He walked to the front double doors with his mouth wide open.

As they entered, it was like a scene from a movie. There was a grand entryway with a large grand staircase leading to the second floor. To the right was a door that led to the sitting room or sun porch. This room led to the biggest kitchen that he had ever seen. This is where he left his mom and dad to talk to the contractor.

Richie kept exploring his new home. He went back through the sun porch and walked to the left side of the house; there was a step-down den. Through another set of double doors was an office/library; this room he knew was his father's. He came back into the entryway and walked behind the staircase, and there were two sets of double doors that led to the backyard. Before he had a chance to see it, his mother wanted him to see the upstairs with her.

So he went sightseeing on the second floor. The first room he entered was a bathroom; it was a nice size. The next two rooms he looked at were guest bedrooms, large and cozy. Then his mom took him to his bedroom; it was beyond words. His room was completely done, even furnished, with a full-size bed, two dressers, a large TV in the corner, a big walk-in closet, and his own bathroom. He was in shock and thanked his mom for his room.

Richie couldn't wait to get in there and make it his room with all his personal things. It was going to be great. She then took him to their bedroom, and it was like a mini house. They had a sitting area, a sleeping area, a dressing area, a walk-in closet to die for, and a fantastic master bath.

Mrs. Ruiz leaned down and said with a laugh, "If by some chance you don't see me or your father for a few days, it's because we got lost in our room—call for help."

Richie looked at his mom and started to laugh. He thought that was funny.

She then showed him the laundry room at the other end of the hall and the entrance to the attic where they will be storing everything that they don't need.

Mrs. Ruiz noticed that Richie was getting bored, so she told him to go and finish exploring the rest of the house. "Oh, and by the way, we will be having some visitors in a little while, so don't get to dirty."

Richie said, "All right, I won't."

As Richie made his way back down the stairs, he went toward the backyard when he spotted another door and peeked in—it was another bathroom. He thought, *How many bathrooms does one house need?* He spotted another door to the right and opened it; this led to the basement. Richie would explore that area at some other time. He had had his share of basements for the time being. When he closed the basement door, he decided to go outside.

When he opened the doors to the backyard, his jaw dropped. There was pool, a pool in his backyard. He couldn't believe it. Along with the pool was a pool house to hold all the toys and equipment used for the pool, and yes, a bathroom and changing area were inside as well.

"Man," Richie said aloud, "they sure know how to build a house."

As he walked around the pool, off to the left was a garden shed to store tools and a mini greenhouse for his mom. She loves to garden and plant her own vegetables. Over to the right on the other side of the pool was a play area that had the standard swing set and other outdoor playthings. Richie looked around and knew they would have more than enough space in this home. He was quite happy.

From his fence he could see Dell's house and Kevin's house. They lived in another subdivision on the other side of the lake. Kevin was outside playing basketball, and Richie yelled to him; however, Kevin was too busy practicing his free throws. When he stopped dribbling the ball, he heard his name and looked around and then he spotted Richie and waved.

Richie waved back, then Kevin shouted, "I will be right over."

Kevin went in to tell his parents he was going to Richie's new house. They said, "All right, be careful." He took off on his bike, even though he could have hopped his fence, took twenty steps around the lake, and be there. He preferred to ride his bike. He enjoyed the cool breeze on his face.

As Kevin was riding by Dell's house, he saw him outside with his mom planting a tree of some sort.

He stopped and asked if Dell could go to Richie's new house with him.

Mrs. McPhearson looked up with dirt on her face and said, "Sure, just be careful."

Dell quickly washed his hands and jumped on his bike, and they both rode toward Richie's new home.

When they arrived, five minutes later, Richie threw open the front door and said in a big booming voice, "Welcome to my new home."

The other two looked at him and said, "Okay, just show us the backyard."

When the other two saw it, they started giving Richie high fives and danced around. "We know where we are spending our weekends at, right, Kevin?" said Dell. "Right here by the pool."

As Richie was showing the boys around the backyard, out comes Mr. Ruiz, Mr. McNeal, and Mr. McPhearson, and they were grinning from ear to ear.

Dell asked them, "What's going on?"

Mr. McPhearson said, "Come with us."

The boys started to follow them to a piece of land that was next door to Richie's house. Mr. McNeal told them, "This piece of property belongs to you three boys. It was donated by the city for you to build your very own clubhouse or whatever you guys want to build." As the boys were yelling and jumping around, Mr. McNeal went over and staked it out with rope and sticks. It was just the right size to build a small building for them to have their detective agency.

The boys told their fathers that they wanted to build a detective agency but don't know how. All three fathers looked at the boys and told them for solving the case that they would build their detective agency with their own hands and money. The boys ran to each of their dads and gave them a hug. Mr. McNeal then pulled out a piece of paper that said that he had taken out a license to run this business, but seeing that he worked full-time, he would leave the business in their capable hands.

The boys were above excited; they were ready to faint.

Then Kevin said, "How did you all know that we wanted to build a detective agency?"

Mr. McPhearson said, "I ran into Sheriff Wilcox Jr. at the post office, and he told me that you guys came and grilled him on what it took to become a detective or something like that. So I called Mr.

McNeal and Mr. Ruiz, and we came up with a plan to try and help you boys accomplish your goals."

The boys looked at each other and then at their own dads and hugged them once again.

Then finally, Mr. Ruiz said, "Since finding sponsors is a hard thing to find, we three have decided to be your sponsors."

"One last thing," said Mr. Ruiz. "Since we are building this with our own money, all you boys have to spend your money on is the furniture to put inside and your equipment. As a bonus we will even install an alarm in the building to protect your things. The only deal is that you three maintain your grades in school and help us one weekend per month till it is completed. It should take us not more than ten weekends to complete, since we all work full-time."

"Can you boys agree to this?" asked the fathers.

All three looked at one another then at their fathers and said, "Yes, sirs, no problem."

They all shook hands and hugged and went inside for lunch that Dell's mom had brought over. She made chicken salad sandwiches, pickles, chips, and punch. The boys and their dads began to eat while the women were still exploring the house. What all the men heard from upstairs were oohs and aahs from their wives. The women joined them after a while, and everyone ate until they were stuffed.

As Richie was heading back to his old house with his folks, he told them that this has been the best summer vacation ever. His mother told him that they were going to start packing this week coming, and he was going to have to go through all his stuff in the bedroom to see what he was taking and what he was giving to the Salvation Army. Richie nodded his head but was kind of sad because he loved his old bedroom and his things. However, the new bedroom in the new house would be just as awesome, and with a few homey touches, it will feel like his old bedroom.

When he got ready for bed that night, he had one more day to spend with his two best friends doing nothing, and he was going to enjoy it.

On Friday morning, all three met at Dell's house to honor their agreement with Dell's dad to help him clean the garage. When Mr. McPhearson came downstairs, all three were waiting for instructions.

Mr. McPhearson looked at all three and said, "The garage can wait for another weekend. Go and relax on your last day of summer vacation before going to school on Monday."

Dell looked at his dad and told him, "You're the best."

The boys then took off riding, thinking that this summer had ended. Their dads were going to start building their agency next weekend. Richie was moving into a new house. Old Man's Harlow's house was being demolished, and the land cleared for a park next to the lake, and life was all right in the little town of Penskee, Wyoming.

However, that would soon change with school starting and a trip that is taken when the boys are off track. This leads to an untold tale of mystery around every corner. They will become intertwined in yet another mystery, *The Secret of the Grandfather Clock.*

The End

About the Author

Marquita grew up with a love for reading from an early age. She discovered The Hardy Boys series, Nancy Drew series, the Trixie Belden mysteries, and Sir Author Conan Doyle, the writer of Sherlock Holmes series. She never tired of reading and trying to solve the fictitious mysteries of these writers. Her imagination led to writing short stories that were based in mystery and intrigue. She grew up to earn her bachelor's degree in education, becoming a schoolteacher, and then later earned her master's degree in social work, becoming a social worker to help families in need. However, her love of storytelling has never left her, and she continued to craft stories from her imaginative brain. Throughout her life, she has been a storyteller, and this adventure hopes to be the first of many. In addition to writing, Marquita loves crafting; watching science fiction/horror from the '50s, '60s, and '70s; and reading books of all genres.